THE SCREW BALL

INDIANAPOLIS LIGHTNING SERIES BOOK 3

SAMANTHA LIND

SAMANTHALIND.COM

Cover Design by Jersey Girl Design
Cover image by FuriousFotog - Golden Czermak
Editing by *Amy Briggs ~ Briggs Consulting LLC*
Proofreading by *Proof Before You Publish*

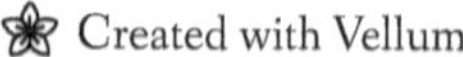 Created with Vellum

CONTENTS

ONE

LUCAS

Titties, titties and more titties.

Every way I look, I see tits. Big ones, small ones, some with dusty nipples, and others with dark-ass ones that could take a man out. I'm not that picky; I like them all. Especially the pair that are inches away from my mouth as the stripper rolls her body to the beat of the music filling the room.

It isn't easy, but I keep my hands to myself. House rules state I cannot touch the girls—pretty standard strip club rules—but they can touch me. The chick in my lap—Candy is what she told me her 'name' was—slides her barley-covered pussy against my hard cock as she pulls my face between her breasts. I can't control myself and lick her skin where she's got my head pinned.

"You like that, sugar?" she asks in what I imagine is the fake-ass sultry voice she uses to entice the guys she does this with on a nightly basis.

"You tell me." I smirk up at her. She damn well can feel just how much I like what she's doing to me.

"I get off in an hour," she states, leaving the rest to my imagination.

"Is that so?" I lick her skin once again, needing another taste of her. I'd like to lick a few other places, but this will have to do for now.

"How much will it cost me for a private hour to finish out your night?" I ask.

"For you," she says, trailing a finger down my chest as she leans back. Her ass is now firmly sitting on my lap with my cock pressed against her. "A grand," she says, her eyes raking back up my body.

"Done," I tell her as I reach into my pocket, pulling out another wad of cash. I watch as her eyes light up while I hand over the Benjamin's. She could have told me it would be five grand, and I would have handed over the cash.

"Now, what did you have in mind?" she asks, tucking the bills inside her corset.

"Whatever you want to do to me. I'm all yours for the next hour."

Candy gets up, strutting her fine-ass body around in front of me as she takes the small and private stage. She expertly swings her body around the pole, dancing to the beat of the music for most of our final hour together.

With about ten minutes to go before the night is over, she struts back over to where I'm sitting and gives me one last lap dance to close out the night.

"It takes me about thirty minutes to change and cash

out, if you want to hang around outside for me," she whispers into my ear before leaving my lap.

I drag my eyes up her body until they lock on hers. My cock has been hard for the last few hours, watching her tease the fuck out of me. Hell yeah, I'll be waiting around for her to get off work so I can actually touch her without getting kicked out of the club.

"I'll be waiting in my car," I tell her, swiping my thumb across my bottom lip. "You live close by?" I ask as an afterthought.

"Yeah, just a few blocks away," she answers before sauntering away. I gather my jacket and hat, sliding my hat on backward before making my way out of the club and to my car.

I slide into the driver's seat and turn it on to blast the air for a few minutes to knock the temperature down a little bit. With the radio playing in the background, I pull my phone out while waiting on *Candy* to finish up her work night, and scroll through Instagram. I usually have a good amount of notifications; people like to tag me in the most random shit. But the amount tonight is a lot higher than it usually is, and I realize why as soon as I click on the first one.

Fuck.

Someone snapped multiple pictures of me while in the club getting lap dances, one with my head between her tits—damn, I miss being in that exact spot right now—but I don't need this shit tonight. I've been trying, as much as the team's PR rep thinks otherwise, to keep myself out of the press since I was called up to Indianapolis.

I flip through some of the comments on the posts. It's a pretty even split of people encouraging me, and those that are disgusted by my actions. I'm a guy; I like tits, so sue me.

I at least am smart enough not to comment on any of the images. Not much I can do about them now that they're out on social media. I'm sure they've already made the rounds on other sites, and come morning, I'm sure I'll hear all about it from my agent and Carmen, the team's PR rep, who I'm pretty sure hates my guts.

"You actually stuck around." A sultry voice pulls me from the distraction on my phone.

"I told you I would, and if I'm anything, it is a man of my word," I tell her as I reach to the dash and turn the music all the way down. "Get in, and we can get out of here."

I watch as Candy walks around the front end of my Lexus SUV. A gift to myself when I got called up and my paychecks got a lot bigger. She opens the passenger door and slides in. Her mini skirt slides up her toned and tanned legs, giving me a lot of skin to look at. I've seen more while inside the club, but there's just something about a woman sitting in the passenger seat of a car that has my blood pumping while the rest of my body is ready to go.

"What way?" I ask once Candy is settled in, and I can pull out of my parking space.

"Take a left out of the parking lot, then a right at the

second light," she instructs. I watch her movements out of the corner of my eye. She's a little fidgety, and I can tell she's a bit nervous, so I reach over and place my palm on her thigh.

"This okay?" I ask. I'd never push myself on any woman. That's not who I am.

"Yeah," she says as I take a right at the second light as she instructed.

"Now what?" I ask once we've turned.

"In about a mile, it will be the large complex on your left. Take the first driveway, and then you can park in any of the spots marked with a visitor sign."

There is hardly any traffic out with the late hour, so we make it to Candy's place petty fast. Her complex is newer from the looks of it. I easily find a spot to park, and then we're both scrambling out of the car and up to her apartment door on the second floor.

"Are you going to tell me your real name?" I ask once we're inside. I lean my back against the closed door as I wait on the answer.

"It's Deborah," she says, turning and smiling at me. She instantly lost the heels she wore when we walked in. Without the height they added to her, she's a tiny thing. One I could break in half, if I'm not careful.

"Deborah." I let her name roll off my tongue. I can see why she'd pick a stage name like Candy. It actually suits her. "Come here." I beckon her closer, giving her the universal come here finger.

"Yes," she coos as she steps into my personal space. Her fingers land on my chest as she slides the tips down my pecs and abs. Even with the layer of fabric from my T-shirt, it feels as if there is nothing between us. I let her explore my body as she wishes. She's already felt me up most of the night, so she knows what I'm packing. I let her unbuckle my belt before pulling the button at the top of my jeans open and sliding the zipper down. I watch as she sinks to her knees and pulls my cock free from my boxers.

My cock twitches in her hand as I watch her tongue flick across her bottom lip, wetting it before she leans forward and does the same to my tip. I draw in a breath as she wraps those perfectly lush lips around my tip and sucks.

I sink my fingers into her hair, pulling it from her face so it doesn't get in the way. I let her keep control of the pace and what she wants to do as she sucks me off. I give a few thrusts of my hips, mainly out of complete pleasure. I've had more blowjobs than I can count, but I can't remember one as good as this, ever.

TWO

CARMEN

"Really, Lucas?" I practically screech across my office. I take in the cocky new outfielder the Lightning called up a couple weeks ago. He's been nothing but a pain in my ass since the moment he arrived. His devilish good looks go hand-in-hand with his playboy personality. "You really thought a night at the strip club was a good idea? Do you know what kind of PR nightmare it creates? Please tell me you didn't actually take the stripper home with you?" I ask, my voice full of disgust.

"For your information," the playboy smirk he's known for—and that apparently makes women's panties just fall at his feet—tugs at his lips. "I didn't take her home; I *never* take women home." He flashes me his full smile.

"That's a plus," I say under my breath.

"She took me home," he follows up, and I can feel my blood pressure rise.

"Fuck!" I growl.

"Feisty, feisty, Red," he smirks again, "just the way I like it."

I turn, placing my fists on my desk as I lean forward. I realize a moment too late that this causes my blouse to hang down, giving him the perfect view right down my top and at my breasts. I can tell by the smirk on his lips that he got an eyeful of my goods, and it pisses me off even more. I stand back up, adjusting my top to take away any possible view of my rack. I suck in a few deep breaths while counting to ten in my head, willing myself to calm down so I can deal with him before I kick him out of my office. "Please do not make assumptions about me, especially anything like that," I sneer.

His eyes rake up and down my body, and I have to will myself from reacting. I absolutely *hate* men like him. Men who think they are God's gift to the world. Who have women falling at their feet for no real reason, except for the pretty face they have, the sport they play, and the bank account that comes along with it.

"Tell me this, Lucas. Why do you purposely do shit to piss me off? And why do you call me Red? I don't have red hair, so it doesn't really fit."

"Well, Carmen." He says my name, letting the R roll off his tongue in a way that has my panties going wet. *Damn him and the havoc he has on my hormones. They need to get with the program that he isn't an option.* I sit down in my chair, allowing me to rub my thighs together discreetly under my desk as I search for a tiny bit of relief. "When you get pissed or excited about something, your cheeks go red," he says, biting his bottom lip as he lets his words sink in. I can feel my cheeks redden even more at his words and the way he's looking at me. He shifts forward in the chair he's sitting in across from me, closing some of the distance between the two of us. "If your cheeks go that red when you're pissed, I can only imagine how red the rest of your body turns, especially when you let loose and come."

"Get out," I growl, pointing at my door as I stand and walk over to it. I can't believe he has the audacity to say something like that to me.

"But I thought you wanted to discuss how you're going to clean up my image?" he retorts, standing and meeting me in the doorway to my office. His eyes rake up my body until they finally make contact with my own. His are full of fire. A fire that will burn me, if I'm not careful.

"I'll do what I can to clean up the current news," I say as professionally as I can, with my blood boiling the way it is. "If you continue to be a dumbass and get yourself into these sticky situations, it's your own doing. If you can't keep yourself out of the press in a bad way, then it is your livelihood it will affect. Sponsors don't want the playboy of the MLB to be the face of their products. The ownership of this team has also invested a lot of money into you, don't make them regret that decision." I remind him, "I can only help you so much; in the end, you've got to help yourself if you really want to change and make a good impression on the ownership. If management isn't happy, they're not going to keep you around; just remember that. Everyone on the team is replaceable."

"I think my play on the field speaks for itself. A few pictures of me out at a strip club every now and again isn't going to have them sending me to another city," he volleys back.

"You're pretty confident for a rookie. I've been around here for a few seasons now. I've seen guys come and go; I wouldn't be so cocky if I were you."

He leans down and whispers into my ear, "I can show you cocky; you just name the time and place." And once again, my blood pressure is up, and my cheeks are flaming hot. What is it about this man that infuriates me while also turning me on to the point I'm about to ruin another pair of panties because of him?

"Go. *Now*," I grit out, doing my best to keep my cool. I take a step back, so I'm entirely in my office and not in my doorway. He gives me one more once over before turning on his heel and heading for the door that will take him from the front offices and into the practice facility.

I shut my office door a little harder than probably necessary, or that's appropriate for an office. But when you put up with the kind of shit like I do with some of the diva players, my patience sometimes quickly runs out.

I take a seat at my desk and quickly type up a press release. After looking it over twice, making some minor edits to it, I send it out to all the appropriate places. While nights out at strip clubs aren't uncommon and really shouldn't be a big deal, they can sometimes spiral out of control. Or, if guys make it a habit, it can create a bad reputation that later comes back to bite them in the ass.

With the headache of Lucas taken care of, I get caught up in an upcoming project management brought to me and asked me to help coordinate. They want to up our community outreach, get involved more with some youth programs and giving back to our great city. While multiple guys work directly with charities that are important to them, the ownership wants something that is specific to the organization as a whole, and that is where I come in.

With my staff's help, we hired an outside planning company to help us pull off this first event.

"Carly, can you come in here, please?" I call out over the intercom to one of my assistants.

"I'll be right there," she says over the speaker.

I move from my desk to the table set up in my office. I love having multiple spaces within my own office to spread out as we're brainstorming ideas. PR isn't always covering up the bad and spinning it to make our clients look good. Sometimes we get to do the fun things and spotlight all the good the team is doing, and that's just what this is going to be.

"Did you get everything with Lucas taken care of?" Carly asks as she enters my office.

"Yes, now if he can keep his nose clean, that will be another thing," I tell her, motioning for her to join me at the table. "I've got some things I wanted your input on for the Fan Fun Days that are coming up," I tell her, pointing at the pages spread out.

"Oh good! I was wondering when these would come

in," she says, taking a seat and looking over what the event company sent for us to review.

The event will consist of kids of all ages participating, spread out over four hours. They'll start the morning getting tours of the facilities, followed by some time out on the field with their favorite players. We've got full range of putting every player to work for this event. Once the field time ends, they'll be led up to the concourse, where we'll be feeding them a baseball staple of hotdogs and chips. We figured most kids would love that. Once they're done eating, they'll be led back down onto the field, where they'll find each player at tables, ready to sign jerseys, T-shirts, hats, or other memorabilia, as well as pose for pictures. All the kids will be moved to the stands, where they'll cheer on the guys as they play a few innings amongst themselves to cap off the event.

"I think the timelines look great. Do we have a head-count, yet?" Carly asks.

"I know we'd discussed having two days, but in the end, we're going with just one for this year. We're completely full with two hundred kids signed up."

"If this goes well, then we can add a second day or session next year."

"I completely agree. I think two hundred for our first year is a good start. It will be hectic, but as long as everyone does as they're assigned, I'm confident we can pull it off."

"Agreed. Just tell me what you need from me next and consider it done," Carly states. She's been a great addition to our team. She started around the beginning of the year and has quickly become my right hand in all things.

"Thanks. I'm going to call Janet and see what they need from us, and then I'll let you know what our next steps are," I tell her, noting that I need to call the event company.

THREE

LUCAS

I stand in the batters' cage, adjust my glove, tap the bat against the ground and then take my spot at the plate. The machine makes a whooshing sound as it sends a fastball my way. I swing, missing the ball completely. I right my stance, ready for the next ball that it sends my way, this time ball and bat connect, and the ball goes flying into the outfield.

"Damn, boy. We need you to hit like that in the game tomorrow night," Justin "JJ" Johnson, our catcher, states, walking up to the cage. He watches as I hit a few more balls.

"That's my plan," I tell him as I take a break, sucking down half of my bottle of Gatorade. It is hot as hell out here today. I've soaked my tank top, so it doesn't do much when I pull up the hem and attempt to mop the sweat off of my face.

"I heard you got on Carmen's shit list," he says, toeing the dirt with his cleat.

"I guess you can say that." I smirk and think back to how hot she was when yelling at me. Seeing her all hot makes me want to see what she'd be like in bed. I start to get hard just thinking of her curvy body pressed against my own. What her skin would feel like under my fingertips. How expertly I could play her body, pulling multiple orgasms from her, all while she's screaming my name. "She wasn't too keen on the fact that I followed a stripper home last night."

"Damn, boy." He laughs, not even hiding it behind the fist pressed to his lips. "Guess someone has to take over my place on the team as the playboy. I was always causing her trouble before my daughter showed up on my doorstep."

"Yeah, what's that all about?" I ask. I never really pay attention to the tabloids and what they're saying about other players. I know how they like to take a picture and run with whatever crazy story they can come up with that they think will sell the article for them.

"Eh, a girl I used to hook up with never bothered to tell me she got pregnant, until she showed up on my doorstep when our daughter was a few weeks old. She'd tried to do it all on her own but realized she wasn't cut out for it, so she brought Evie to me. It's been a whirlwind few months, but the best months ever, at the same time. She's everything I never knew I needed in my life; and she also brought me the love of my life, so like I said, it's all been for the best. Kinda funny how things work out that way."

"I don't think I'd look at that situation the same way,"

I tell him honestly. "Plus, the thought of settling down with one woman gives me hives. Women equal drama," I state.

"Six months or a year ago, I would have agreed with you, one-hundred percent. But when the right woman drops into your lap, you'll know it. She won't like you or want you because of the uniform you put on, or the car you drive, or the connection you can get her for her social media following. She'll like you for you. For the way you treat her and the way that you only let your guard down for her. When you make her feel special and like she's the center of your world, she'll do the same to you."

"Aren't you dating Derek's sister or something like that?"

"Yep," he says, popping the p before continuing on. "Riley came to my rescue when Evie was dropped off. Like, dropped everything and moved into my house to help me. I didn't know my ass from my elbow when it came to babies, and Evie was less than a month old when she arrived. Riley had been a nanny before and knew exactly what to do. Whatever she didn't know, Derek's wife, Jillian, was right there to answer. We both fought the connection for as long as we could, but in the end, we decided to see what came of it, and well, it's the best decision we've made." He gushes, all in love like. It almost makes me want to puke.

"Sounds like a messy situation."

He laughs at my comment. "It was definitely messy." Our attention gets pulled for a few seconds to a group of guys that are all laughing as they come out of the dugout and onto the field. "Have you gotten all settled in, now that you've been here a few weeks?" JJ asks.

"Yep, got all moved in to my apartment. I've been exploring the city when I can, finding the best places to blow off steam, if you know what I mean." I smirk, knowing that he damn well knows what I'm talking about.

"Yeah, I heard all about you blowing off steam." He chuckles. "Just keep yourself out of the spotlight, and you can blow off all the steam you want," he adds.

"I can't help it if the camera loves me." I strike a pose for the pretend photographer.

"An attitude like that will do nothing but get you into trouble, and being in trouble will forever keep you on Carmen's shit list," JJ says.

"What's her deal?" I ask, hoping that my interest isn't glaringly apparent.

"Don't even think about it," he warns. "She isn't your type, or better yet, you aren't hers."

"I was just wondering why she's always so pissed off or acting like she's got a stick up her ass."

"When you cause problems she's got to clean up, you aren't going to see her fun and friendly side. Maybe try doing something that brings you good publicity and see how she reacts."

"Eh, what's the fun in that?" I joke. "I'll be honest, I kind of like seeing her all worked up."

"Keep those thoughts to yourself." He barks out a laugh. "She'll be the first one to put you in your place if you try and come on to her," he warns.

"I'll take that as a challenge."

"Whatever, man, just don't go pissing her off. You make the entire team's lives miserable; we'll make your life miserable. Understand?" he asks, giving me a stern glare.

"Got it," I tell him. I don't have any plans on pissing off the rest of my team. I worked my ass off to get called up; no way I want to piss anyone off and have them sending me back down.

I STEP OUT ONTO THE FIELD AND LOOK AROUND AT the empty stadium. It won't be long and the gates will be opened, and the fans will fill all the seats. I remember back to the first time I ever played in a stadium this large. It wasn't anything compared to playing for the Lightning, but it was still an incredible experience. I was in college when it happened, now playing here is always special. I'm used to the big lights and the sounds of the massive crowds.

I run a few laps around the outfield as I warm my body up in my pre-game ritual. I've fine-tuned what works best for me over the years, changing up little things here and there that help me play to the best of my abilities. The last thing I want to happen is to get hurt bad enough I end my career before it ever has time to really take off. I've put in way too many early mornings and late nights staying up to practice to throw it all away now that I have my future and dreams in the palm of my hand.

I wipe the sweat from my face, the afternoon sun beating down on me. I'm hopeful the temps will dip a little once the sun goes down and isn't shining directly on the field with an evening game. I look over to the dugout and see a few people milling about. A few other guys are out here stretching and warming up. The grounds crew is out perfecting the dirt, lining the field with the chalk lines, and putting in the bases before the game. I notice Carmen talking to a few people I don't recognize, pointing to different parts of the field, and now my curiosity has piqued. What are they discussing? Is she really having to explain the game and where players spread out to on the field? I pick up my glove, ball, and water bottle and head back toward where she's standing. I have to pass right by them to head back inside to the locker room so I can get dressed in my uniform and ready for the official warmups before the game.

"Lucas," Carmen greets me as I approach. The disdain practically drips from her voice as she says my name.

"Carmen," I greet in return and watch her reaction from behind my polarized sunglasses. I know she can't see my eyes behind these lenses, which allows me full range of taking in her luscious curves. What I wouldn't do to get her under me, or on top of me, or hell, against a wall for all I care. There is just something about this woman that drives me fucking crazy. "I didn't realize giving tours was part of the PR department's job." I smirk.

"I'm not giving a tour; we're going over station placement for the Fan Fun Day that is next week," she informs me. "Don't forget. Everyone is required to attend and help. You'll have a specific job that day, so don't screw it up," she says, turning to face me fully as she stands her ground. I take a small step forward, effectively closing the gap between us. I don't have any intentions of touching her since she's in her business attire while I'm standing here sweaty in a tank and basketball shorts.

"Sorry, what day is that again? I might have made other plans," I state, just to piss her off some more.

"It is on Thursday. I don't care what other plans you might think you've made; cancel them. This isn't negotiable," she grits between clenched teeth.

I hold up my hands, palms out, as if I'm going to hold her back from attacking me. "Damn, I was joking," I tell her. "I don't have any plans that day, and I'll make sure to be here." I pause long enough to take a drink of my water. "I'll even show up early if that will make you feel better," I offer.

"You're such an ass," she says, giving me a smile that I know anyone else would think was sweet or friendly, but I can tell standing just inches from her that it is anything but sweet or nice, and that has me thinking once again what her lips would look like wrapped around my cock. *Fuck, I can't be thinking about that while on the field.*

"I aim to please," I toss out as I step away and head down the few steps into the dugout and then inside.

I head straight for the locker room, where I find most of my teammates milling around in a mixture of half-dressed states. I pull the tank I had on from my body, wiping at my torso with the fabric to wipe away some of the sweat that is still on my skin. Before getting my uniform on, I hit up the bathroom, then head back to my locker to get dressed.

Many athletes have a specific system. They might always put on their left sock before the right, or always eat a particular meal before every home game or run a specific number of lines across a field. I've done all of those things myself at one point or another, and today is no different. I started with my warmup; now it is time to get my uniform on in a particular order. Clean compression shorts followed by a compression tank to help with the sweat. My uniform pants come next, followed by my socks, then my top, and finally my cleats. Always done in that order. I snag my hat before leaving my locker, sliding it on my head as I head out of the locker room and into the dugout.

FOUR

CARMEN

I rush around the stadium, making sure everything is where it is needed. The guys have started to arrive, which I'm thankful for. I've stressed myself out over the fact that some of them might skip today and make things not go to plan. The day is young, so I'm not counting out something might still go against my well-thought-out plan, but I'm also hoping that everything goes smoothly.

"Carmen, did you want me to take these bags down to the dugout?" my assistant Carly asks.

"Yes, please. I think Derek and Justin are here already, so if you need some muscle, I'm sure they'd be willing to help you," I tell her, mentioning one of our star pitchers and catchers for the team. They also happen to be best friends, and it won't surprise me if they end up being brothers-in-law, since Justin is dating Derek's sister, and I think things are pretty serious between the two of them.

"I'll see who I can round up," Carly calls before she grabs a box of the goodie bags we've put together for all the kids to take home at the end of the day filled with team swag, and heads for the tunnel that will lead her out to the dugout.

I head up to the concourse to check in with catering to ensure they've got everything in place for lunch today. I'm sure I have nothing to worry about; it isn't like they aren't used to a packed stadium with upwards of forty-plus thousand people here each and every game.

All is good with catering, so I head back down to wait for everyone to arrive. We'd asked the players to get here an hour before fans will be let in, mainly so I can go over with them what their duties will be and a quick overview of the day's events. They were already given most of this information, but I've learned that some guys don't retain these types of instructions for long. So, I just planned to go over everything beforehand; that way, no one is surprised about anything happening over the next few hours.

"Janet, is everything set up on the field how you wanted?" I ask the coordinator from the event company we hired to help us pull today's event off. Like me, she's been running around all morning, making sure things are in place.

"It is all perfect; we just need some kids now to fill it up," she says, her excitement causing her to bounce on the balls of her feet.

"Perfect! I can't thank you enough for all of your help

with this. I think it will be a fantastic event for us to continue for years to come."

"I think you're right. The kids are going to love it, and I believe the guys will have more fun than they imagine."

"Carmen," Ian Rogers, the team manager, calls my name from the doorway of his office. I turn on my heel and head his way.

"Yes, Ian?" I ask in greeting when I reach his office.

"Did you want to give your speech to the guys now?" he asks. "We're only missing a couple of them, but I'm sure they'll be here soon."

"Of course," I tell him, and he leads me down the hall and into the locker room where they've all congregated.

This isn't my first time in the locker room; I'm actually in here quite often. As the team's lead PR person, I deal with the media daily. Many of them have access to this very room, but only when I give the green light that they can enter. We also have a time limit they can spend in here with the guys. It works really well, and most of the media abide by those boundaries. We have a few that like to test the limits, but all it takes is me revoking their pass for one game, and they shape up pretty quickly.

I look around the room, finding all but three of the locker bays filled with one of the guys. All of them did as requested and are wearing team-issued clothing. I didn't think that was a hardship, seeing how many different items they are given.

Two of the three empty lockers don't surprise me, as they are for guys that are out injured, and they were given the option to be here today, rather than it being mandatory. The one that has my blood pressure rising is none other than my thorn of a player, Lucas Black.

Ian must realize my assessment of who is missing, as he's quick to speak up. "I've called Lucas already, telling him he needs to get his ass here. So far, he hasn't replied, but I assure you, he'll be appropriately disciplined for missing a mandatory team event."

"Of course he isn't here," I mutter under my breath. "Thanks for that; I'll make sure his station gets covered until he arrives," I tell Ian.

I watch as he slinks away, probably to go call Lucas again. I don't know why I believed him when he told me he'd be here and on time. I guess, fool me once, shame on him. I won't let him fool me twice, that's for sure.

I quickly go over everything with the guys. What I'm asking them to do isn't much different than any other fan event; this one just happens to have everyone here at once rather than just a few of them at an hour-long appearance.

Before I know it, the first few hours have passed by in a blur of laughter and fun. Everywhere I look, kids are having a blast, as are the players. Lucas still hasn't shown up, and the last I heard from Ian, he won't be here anytime soon. I'm not sure what was so important, but Ian assured me that he's dealing with the situation and I don't need to worry about it. That has my mind spinning, wondering what trouble he's gotten himself into and what mess I'll be cleaning up in the press later today or tomorrow.

We lead the kids up to the concourse and through the

lines so they can all get their lunches. Much like down on the field, this space is filled with so much chatter and laughter that I can't wipe the smile off my face at what we've accomplished today.

"Hey, Carmen," Derek Smyth calls out from down the hall once almost everyone has left. I stop and turn in his direction as he approaches.

"What can I do for you, Derek?" I ask, giving him a polite smile.

"I just wanted to tell you how much fun I had today. As wary as I was about having so many kids here at once, it was a really well-planned out and executed event, all thanks to you," he compliments.

"Th-Thank you." I get a little choked up at his praise. "I really appreciate it. I hope that we can continue this each year," I tell him honestly.

"After today's event, I don't see why it can't happen. Did you see the smiles on all those kids' faces? Hell, even all the guys had smiles plastered on all day."

"I did, plus, we got some great video and photographic evidence of it," I tell him. "Thanks for believing in me. We took an idea and ran with it. I'm just grateful that it turned out as good as it did."

I make small talk with Derek for a few more minutes. He fills me in on how his daughters are doing, as well as his wife. He's got a cute little family, and I'm happy for him that he didn't lose it all when they had a slight bump in the road last year. Sometimes it takes hitting rock bottom for people to realize everything they have and how important it is to make changes they need.

FIVE

LUCAS

I load another fifty pounds onto the barbell before assuming the position so the bar can rest across my shoulders. I lift it off of the rack, getting my feet set correctly before I start my set of squats. I'm already halfway through my workout for the morning and feeling pretty good today.

"Lucas!" I hear my name being barked from the doorway. I almost missed it since I've got my earbuds in and music pumping to keep my focus. I finish my set of ten squats before placing the bar back on the stand behind me. I grab the towel I have draped on the bench, wiping at my face as I walk toward the door and the two people standing there waiting on me.

If looks could kill, I'd be six feet under the ground already, based on the daggers Carmen is shooting at me. I know I messed her little event up yesterday, but I had more important things to deal with, things she doesn't need to know about. I already talked to coach about it, and he understood my reasoning for missing it. While I know it wasn't a smart move to not call him beforehand and to go so long before I returned his many calls, he didn't bench me or send me back down to the AAA team, so I'm taking that as a plus in my book.

Before either of them can start talking, I decide to control this conversation from the get-go. "Listen, I'm sorry I missed the event yesterday. Coach and I have already talked it out. I know it was an asshole move to miss, but I had something come up that I couldn't get out of that was more important," I tell her without giving her any details about what I was doing yesterday. It doesn't pertain to her or the team; therefore, I don't feel the need to share my day's details.

"It was mandatory," she seethes, and that pretty red shade I love seeing her skin turn makes an appearance. I can't help but smirk, thinking back to our conversation in her office not long ago when she asked me why I call her Red occasionally.

"And I'm sorry, Red." I smirk again when the nickname slips from my lips and the daggers become even more intense. Damn, someone needs to pin this woman against a wall and fuck her until she can't think straight. "But as I said, I had something personal come up that I couldn't get out of," I tell her, staying as calm as can be as I try and hide the fact that her being all pissed at me is turning me the fuck on.

"Carmen, I can vouch for Lucas. While we can't guarantee that the same thing won't happen again, we did come to the agreement that if he's tied up with this matter again, he'll reach out to me before he's supposed to be somewhere and let me know what's going on."

I watch as she digests his words. Her level of disgust with me appears to change as the wheels in her mind start turning as she starts to wonder what it was that Coach is so easy to let me off the hook for.

"I guess if you're okay with this behavior, I have no choice but to go with your decision," Carmen says to Ian.

I watch as she turns and walks down the hallway. I can't help but observe the way her hips sashay down the hall in her tight pencil skirt. That tight ass would feel amazing pressed up against my groin as I pound into her from behind. *Fuck, there goes my mind again.*

"Are you good for tonight's game?" Coach asks, pulling my thoughts from stripping Carmen from her clothes.

"Yeah, I'm good," I tell him. I run a hand around my neck, squeezing the tight muscles, hoping that they'll loosen up some before the game.

"You look tense; maybe go visit one of the therapists to see if they can get that out of you."

"Will do, I've got a few things to finish up in the weight room, and then I can check with them," I tell him, pointing my thumb over my shoulder at the door we're standing outside of.

"You're a good player and a good kid. Don't forget that, now," he tells me before walking off down the hall toward the team offices.

I try not to think about the events yesterday, if I focus

on them too much, they will affect my play, and none of us need that right now.

It's the bottom of the ninth, and we're down by one run. We've got a runner on second when I step up to the plate. I tighten the strap on my glove, tap the end of my bat against home plate and take my stance as I watch the pitcher go through his head shakes as the catcher flashes him ball signals until he lands on one he likes, followed by his throwing routine before the ball leaves his fingertips and is headed my way at over ninety miles per hour. I stay still, not flinching as the catcher has to lean to the side to catch the stray ball. I hear the umpire call the ball before we all reset. This pitcher hasn't been on the mound long and isn't having the greatest night so far. He gave up a home run with his first batter, JJ, followed by a fly ball that went deep into the outfield by Matt O'Riley, one of our first basemen.

I watch as he goes through the same routine, this time changing up what he's sending my way. Unfortunately for him, he places it perfectly, and the ball loudly cracks against my bat as I send it sailing high into the air as it floats further and further away. I take off like a bat out of hell, quickly rounding first as Matt clears home plate, tying the game for us. My ball continues to fly, eventually going out of the field and into the stands, giving me my first ever MLB home run of my career. I slow my running slightly as I take in the crowd's loud sounds as they are all cheering at the top of their lungs as they stand on their feet. As I approach home plate, I'm met by my entire team as they join me to celebrate our win.

"What are you doing to celebrate the win tonight?" Matt calls out across the locker room once all the media has been kicked out by Carmen so that we can get on with our evening and get showered and changed.

"Nothing planned; what did you have in mind?" I ask him.

"We could hit up a club; I've got nothing else going on," he suggests.

"Sounds good to me; I'll grab my shower now," I tell him, pulling out my bag from my locker. I remove the last of my compression clothes and wrap a towel around my waist before heading for one of the showers.

I walk out of the locker room, looking fresh and ready to hit the club. While I hadn't planned to head to one after the game, the clothes I brought with me to change into are appropriate enough to hit up a club in. I've got on dark-washed jeans with a polo that pulls tightly across my chest and around my biceps. Not many shirts can hide these guns.

"Lucas," Carmen's sugary sweet yet annoyed voice greets my ears. "Nice way to close out the game tonight," she says, standing just a foot or so away from me. My eyes quickly drop down her body, taking in her casual yet professional attire. While she's changed out of the pencil skirt and blouse she was in this morning, she's now in a team polo shirt and some khaki shorts.

"Thanks, it was a pretty sweet hit."

"Your first home run, I'd say that's something to cele-brate." She smiles up at me, and I feel like this is the first-ever genuine smile she's given me.

"Yep," I say, popping the p. "Matt and I are headed out to celebrate," I tell her.

"For the love of everything holy, please don't do anything that requires me to clean up a mess," she says, rolling her eyes.

I chuckle; she makes it seem like all I do is get into trouble, when in reality, I've only had the press on me about things a couple times, and only one was so-called wrong, with the strip club incident. "Got it. I'll keep things PG tonight while in the public eye. I can't say the same once I'm out of the club though." I run my teeth along my bottom lip and watch as her eyes dilate at the movement. *Hmm...maybe I'm not the only one who gets turned on in this little twosome.*

"Can you not keep it in your pants for one night?" she scoffs.

"Wouldn't you like to know?" I smirk, and her eyes roll once again.

"Ready to go, man?" Matt asks, stepping out of the locker room. "Oh, hey, Carmen. How are you tonight?" he asks her, pulling her into a side hug. I have to stop myself from growling at his easiness with her and hers with him. *Where the hell did that possessiveness come from?*

"I'm good, ready to get out of here. It's been a long couple of days," she tells him as they separate.

"Don't let me keep you, then," he says, slapping a

hand on my shoulder. "I'm taking this guy out to celebrate that hit tonight. I think it deserves a drink or two," he tells her.

"Have fun, don't do anything stupid," she tells him, then shoots daggers at me again.

"You know I'd never," he says, acting like he's some squeaky-clean choir boy who isn't ready to hit the club, looking for someone to take home for the night.

"Night, guys," she says as a final farewell before heading down the hall. I can't help but watch as she walks away, that ass once again teasing me until I'm hard in my jeans.

"Don't even think about it," Matt warns. "She isn't the one-night stand kind of girl. Plus, I think she might be a little out of your league," he cracks.

"Funny." I chuckle as we both head for the exit.

"Meet you at the club?" he calls out, opening his driver's door. He drives a little sporty Audi.

"Sounds good to me," I tell him, opening the door to my Lexus SUV.

I walk up to the club entrance with Matt by my side. Since it is a Friday night, a short line has started to form, but that's not a problem for us. The bouncer at the door recognizes both of us instantly, offering out his fist for us to bump.

"Evening, guys, I didn't know you were coming down tonight," he says, opening the rope for us to step through. I catch the look from a few of the young women standing at the front of the line as they rake their eyes all over my body. Yeah, they like what they see.

"We've got some celebrating to do," Matt tells him. "This guy hit his first professional home run, and it was a walk-off winner, at that."

"Damn, congratulations, man," the bouncer says, slapping my shoulder.

"Thanks," I tell him as the door to the club opens. The music pours from the open doors as we step through, then immediately head up the stairs to the VIP lounge. While I don't mind hanging out in the central area, being that it is a Friday night, the VIP lounge is probably a better place for us to be. Plus, they'll have a better liquor selection and prettier bartenders.

"Evening, gentlemen, I'm Savannah; what can I get the two of you tonight?" one of the servers asks as we approach a table.

"Whiskey on the rocks," Matt tells her, then points to me as if he's asking what I want to drink. "First round is on me," he says.

"In that case, I'll take a bottle of Dom Perignon," I tell the server.

"Right away, gentlemen." She smiles at both of us and heads straight for the bar to put in our order.

"Fucker, I see how it is; had to order an entire bottle when it's my tab." He chuckles.

"Damn straight," I tell him. I look out over the dance floor, eyeing a few groups of girls that I'll keep a watch on to see if anyone might be interested in some company. I need to get laid. It's been a few weeks since I went home with that stripper, and I need some release.

"I've got your drinks here for you. Did either of you

want to order anything from the kitchen?" she offers. Only the VIP lounge at this club provides a small kitchen with some appetizer-style offerings.

"I'm good for now," I tell her as Matt also waves her offer off. "Thanks." I flash her a smile, the one that I know drops women's panties at my feet. The lights might be dimmed in here, but I can still see the blush her cheeks flush and know that she'll be putty in my hands before the night is over, if I want.

"If either of you needs anything else, just flag me down," she says, stepping away then stopping at the next table to check on them.

"To your first of many home runs," Matt says, holding up his tumbler of Whiskey to clink against my flute of champagne. I swallow down the small amount of bubbly goodness, the bubbles tickling my nose slightly. I top my glass off from the bottle our server placed in an ice bucket next to the table and tip it back just as quickly as I did the first.

"You on the prowl tonight?" I ask Matt once we've both enjoyed the majority of our first drinks. We're both surveying the club and those in attendance tonight.

"Maybe, just taking in the options for the evening." He smirks, checking out a girl that just walked into the VIP area. Her dress doesn't leave much to the imagination and I can tell Matt is interested, for sure. He perks up as his eyes follow her every move across the room until she stops at the bar. "I'll be right back," he tells me quickly and I watch as he slides up to the bar next to the knock-out beauty.

I watch the interaction from our table for a minute or so. It is hard to determine if things are going well since I can only see their backs, but he's standing next to her, their bodies angled slightly toward one another. He must be laying on the charm based on her body language. A slide of her fingertips along his forearm, followed by his hand sliding along her waist, until it rests just above her ass as he pulls her a little closer.

"Can I get you another drink?" our server asks, pulling my attention from my teammate and friend.

"A bottle of water would be great; do you have any?" I ask, knowing I need to slow my alcohol intake. Not only because I need to get myself home, but also because I don't want to deal with a hangover tomorrow.

"Of course," she says, flashing me a cute smile that I am sure is her way of telling me she's available. She's cute enough and I was once feeling the need to hook up tonight, but the more I look around, the more that desire isn't prevalent. Not sure what the hell is up with that, but maybe I'm just tired and need to head home for a good night's sleep.

I look around the lounge, spotting Matt still wrapped up in his conversation turned make-out session with the chick at the bar.

"Thanks for this," I say, grabbing the bottle of water she delivered to me. The cold liquid quenches my thirst as she stands close by, I'm sure, hoping I'll ask her out.

SIX

CARMEN

I roll over in bed, stretching my arms above my head as I do most mornings. I reach for my phone as per my usual ritual. I wasn't woken up to deal with anything overnight, which is a true blessing. But I still make it a priority to check all my notifications right away each morning to not miss anything important that might have transpired.

With no pressing issues, I take a few minutes to scroll through my personal account. I stop to look through the album of pictures my sister-in-law posted of my nephew. He's the cutest damn kid, sporting two new teeth in his otherwise gummy smile. I drop a few hearts on the pictures. It's moments like this, seeing him growing up through pictures and the occasional FaceTime that I wish we lived closer, but with my brother being in the military, that won't be a possibility until he's out of the service and can decide where they're going to call home for good.

I finally drag my butt out of bed after scrolling for another twenty or so minutes, thanks to my bladder screaming at me that it is time to get moving. Before leaving the bathroom, I wash my face and brush my teeth. Checking the clock, I see I have just enough time to make it to my favorite yoga studio for one of my favorite Saturday morning classes.

Feeling slightly refreshed and excited for a much-needed class, I pull on some shorts, a sports bra and a tank top before sliding into some sandals. I fill a bottle with some ice water, grab a banana from the counter, along with my keys and cell, and head out the door. I love my condo building, as it is in a pretty up and coming area that has been revitalized over the last few years. I have so many places I can go within walking distance.

A short, five-or-so-minute walk later and I'm striding through the doors of the yoga studio. I toss my banana peel in the trash before placing my items in one of the small lockers they have in the lobby for customers. After getting all checked in, I grab a mat and pick a place in the open room. I lay down, starting a few stretches to get me warmed up before the class actually starts.

An hour later, I'm a puddle of sweat and feeling so much better. There is just something about a good yoga session that centers me and helps me relax. With a constantly go-go-go mentality at work, I sometimes have a hard time shutting my brain off and relaxing, but yoga makes me tune everything out for the hour I'm in the studio, sweating my ass off and finding the calm I so desperately need most days.

After cleaning my mat off and putting it back in the pile, I gather my phone and keys from the locker, then make my way outside. The sun is bright, making today a gorgeous day. I stop at the coffee shop on the corner, ordering an iced latte and breakfast wrap to go. I eat the wrap on the short walk back home, finishing it quickly since I was starving after my class and only ate a banana on the way.

I step out of the shower, wrapping my hair up first before toweling off, and then wrapping my fluffy towel around my body. My cell starts to buzz against the counter. I grab it, seeing that Carly is calling.

"Hello," I greet, putting her on speaker right away.

"Hey! What are you up to today?" she asks.

"I don't have any plans yet, went to yoga this morning and just getting dressed for the day now. What are you up to?"

"Do you want to meet up down at the farmers' market?" she asks.

"I'd love to," I tell her, knowing that it is going to be a beautiful day and I need to restock my fridge with some fresh fruits and veggies. "Does in an hour work for you?" I ask, seeing as how I'm in a towel.

"That will be perfect. John and I will meet you there," she says before disconnecting.

With a place to be, I get moving. I turn on a random play list and connect my phone to my Bluetooth speaker. I pull out a red sun dress to put on, then get to working on my hair. I pull it up and off my neck, braiding it into a twist that will help keep me cool in the hot, late-summer sun. With just a few swipes of mascara and some Chapstick, I'm ready to take on the day. I love it when I have a down day and don't feel like I have to put on a full face of makeup. I'm not like most girly girls who can't even go to the gym without a full face of makeup. If I had things my way, I wouldn't wear it every day to work, but people frown upon looking washed out and tired all the time.

It doesn't take me the full hour to get ready, but the farmers' market is not within walking distance, I've got a good ten-to-fifteen-minute drive across town to get there, depending on the traffic, and with Indianapolis traffic, you never know what you're going to get.

I circle around, finally finding a parking spot on the street a few blocks away. With free parking on the weekends, street spots are a rarity to come across and it is basically luck to find one. I happen to see the people who just left walking to their car while I was stopped at the light a block away, so I was able to snag it as soon as the light changed, and they pulled away.

I grab my reusable shopping bags, clipping them onto my cross-body bag I brought with me today. I head the few blocks down to the market, finding a bench to sit on while I wait for Carly and her boyfriend, John, to make it here. I shoot off a text letting her know where she can find me once they find a place to park.

"Thanks for the invite," I tell her once we've walked down the first row of booths.

"Of course! I figured if I didn't get you out of the house, you'd probably get lost in something boring like cleaning the bathroom. Couldn't pass up this beautiful day and fresh food." She chuckles, and it is scary how well she knows me.

"My walk this morning to and from yoga had me ready for some more outdoor time, so this is perfect. Plus, it takes care of restocking my fruits and veggies for the week."

"I'm so excited for all the things that are finally available now that we're nearing the end of summer," Carly muses as we stop at a few of the booths. A lot of the stands offer the same basic items, all your basic veggies and some fruits. Some offer additional baked goods or local honey, along with hand crafted items at other booths. I quickly fill my bags with fixings for salads and a stir-fry I plan to make later this week, as well as some in-season fruits to have with my breakfasts or to take with me to work for a healthy snack mid-afternoon. If I take healthy options, it usually keeps me from hitting up the breakroom vending machines for a chocolate bar, which my hips definitely don't need on a daily basis.

"What are you guys up to tonight?" I ask Carly and John as I sit across from them at a picnic table. The market also features a row of food trucks. Once we were done perusing the booths, it was lunchtime, so we grabbed something.

"A friend of mine from high school is a comedian and on tour. He's got a show tonight and we're going to go see him perform," John says.

"Oh, that sounds like fun!"

"He's pretty great! Was on one of those comedy shows on TV last year. Made it to the final three contestants before he was sent home," Carly tells me.

"Wow, that's pretty cool. I hope you guys have fun."

"What are you doing tonight?" she asks.

"Not sure yet, I don't have any plans. I'll probably prep some meals for the week, then maybe curl up with a book and glass of wine."

"You should get a ticket and come with us," Carly suggests.

"Oh, I'd never want to crash your date night," I push back at the idea. I hate feeling like the third wheel when I do things with my friends who are in a relationship.

"It isn't crashing if we invite you," she states.

"I can text my buddy and see if he knows if any ticket is still available, if you want," John offers.

I worry my bottom lip as I think over their offer. On one hand, doing something out of my house and around other people that isn't work related sounds fun. "What the hell, it doesn't hurt to ask," I give in.

"Yay!" Carly cheers as John's fingers start to fly across the screen of his phone as he texts his friend.

"He said the only tickets left are the ones that he can give out, so he'll leave one at will call for you to get."

"Oh, I'm more than willing to pay for it. I didn't need a free one," I insist.

"It isn't a problem. All venues give him a handful of tickets, they don't always go to anyone. He said it wasn't a problem at all."

"Will I be able to sit with you guys?" I ask, not really wanting to be by myself or sat with a table full of strangers.

"Yeah, the place it is at is all general admission tickets, so as long as we arrive together, they'll seat us together. Plus, with us all having tickets directly from Mike, we might be seated in the front VIP section. He wasn't sure when I was texting him the other day," John tells me.

"Okay, then! What time does the show start?" I ask.

"Nine, doors open at eight. Want to grab dinner before?" Carly suggests.

"Absolutely, my treat," I tell them.

"Oh, you don't have to do that," John tries to argue.

"No, I insist. You are letting me crash your date night, you got me a free ticket, so it is the least I can do, really," I tell him.

"I'm not going to argue with you, but at least let us pick up the tip or something," he offers.

"We'll see," I say to pacify him.

"We were thinking of hitting up The Garage Food Hall. Some of the guys were talking about it at work the other day and said the food there was really good. I looked up the menu and from the sound of it, I'd have to agree with them," Carly says.

"Sounds good. Should we plan to meet there at, like, six thirty? That gives us a little cushion of time in case we have to wait for a table," I suggest.

"That works for us," Carly confirms.

We finish up our lunches before parting ways until it is time to meet again this evening for dinner and the show.

SEVEN

LUCAS

I walk out of the locker room and into the hallway that will lead me to a multitude of places within the facility or out to the players' parking lot.

After this morning's weight session, followed by practice, I'm ready for a hot meal and a decent night's sleep. We take off in the morning for a week-long road trip that includes four games, so I also need to get packed tonight, as we're wheels up at eight in the morning.

"Mr. Black," I hear my name being called from down the hall. I turn, seeing one of Carmen's assistants headed my way, so I stop and wait for her to catch up to me.

"What can I do for you, Carly, is it?" I ask, not missing the eye roll she gives me.

"Yes, it is Carly," she says, kind of snotty. Who pissed in this girl's Cheerios this morning? "We had a request come in from a children's hospital in Tampa with a request from a patient who is a fan of yours. They were wondering if you'd be willing to come by when the team is in town and see the child. He's in the middle of a pretty rough chemotherapy regimen and they think it might boost his spirits."

"Yeah, can you get it all set up? I should be able to go over on Wednesday morning for a little while as long as you get it cleared with Coach," I tell her. I'm almost always willing to give my time, especially in a situation like this.

"Thank you," she says, and I think I shocked her at how easily I agreed to the request. Little does she know; I'd never turn a request like this away. The kids don't deserve to be sick and in the hospital, so if an hour of my time will help them, then why not? "I'll get everything approved and set up, including a car to take you to and from the hospital, either from the stadium or the hotel, wherever you'll be at that time," she says, which is a good thing since the team is always transported by motor coach once we make it to a city. I could always take an Uber, but having a prearranged car is probably for the best.

"Can you text me the details once you have them finalized?" I ask, knowing that the office has all of the players' numbers.

"Of course. Would you like to take anything with you?" she asks. "The team can donate some items for you to give."

"Yeah." I take my baseball cap off, running my fingers through my hair, making me realize I need to fit in a cut today, as well, before I place it on my head backward.

"Whatever you can put together will be good. I've got some errands to run, but can swing back by before I head home."

"I can do that, or I can send it with the equipment manager," she offers.

"That works for me," I tell her, liking that option better.

"Will do, I'll still text you once we have everything confirmed with the hospital."

"Thanks," I tell her before we part ways. It's almost a shame that it wasn't Carmen who relayed that information to me. I love getting every chance I can to razz her up, but alas, today isn't one of those days.

I pull out of the parking lot, my windows all rolled down to let the fresh air in. The early September breeze is finally cooling it down just a little bit outside. We've only got a couple weeks left before the post season starts, which I'm looking forward to.

I'm cruising down the interstate when something catches my eye in the rearview mirror. *Fuck*, flashing lights on the cop car behind me.

I flip on my blinker, slowing to a stop on the shoulder of the road. Once stopped, I place my SUV into park, and reach for my registration and insurance card as the officer approaches my car.

"License and registration," she requests from the open window.

I hand over the requested documents. "Can you tell me why you pulled me over, officer?" I ask.

"Clocked you going eighty-five in a sixty-five zone," she states, matter-of-factly. "Where are you headed in such a hurry, Mr. Black?" she asks, using my last name after she's had the chance to look over my information. I can't see her eyes, as she's got on polarized sunglasses, so I can't tell if she knows who I am outside of reading my driver's license.

"Just out doing some errands before I head home," I tell her. "I didn't realize I was even going that fast, was just kind of moving along with traffic," I tell her honestly.

"It is easy to do that sometimes," she says. "Since I don't see anything else suspicious, I'm going to let you go with just a warning. Slow it down and pay attention to the posted signs, especially the speed ones," she tells me, and I sigh in relief that I'm not getting a ticket. One less thing to put me on Carmen's shit list.

I make my way out of the hotel and into the waiting town car. Carly came through with all the logistics for the hospital visit. I've got a bag filled with items to donate to the young boy who I'm going to see. I can only hope that my visit today and the items I have for him help, even if it's temporary.

"The drive to the hospital isn't long," the driver tells me as we pull out of the hotel's parking lot.

"No problem, I don't think they're expecting me for another twenty or so minutes," I tell the older gentleman.

He must be used to driving people who don't want to talk, not that I mind much. I watch as the buildings and palm trees zoom past as we make our way. As he predicted, the drive only took about ten minutes.

"I'll drop you at the front doors, then wait for you in the back of the parking lot. On your way down, send me a text," he states and hands over a business card, "to the number on this card and I'll pull around and pick you back up at the door I dropped you off at."

"Will do," I tell him, tucking the card into my pocket. I grab the bag the team sent with me before exiting the car and heading inside.

"Hello, how can I help you?" the older woman at the information desk asks when I approach.

"Hello, I'm Lucas Black. I'm here to see Tyler Grub, he's in the pediatric oncology ward. Can you point me in that direction, please?"

"Of course, Mr. Black," she says, smiling up at me after she types something into the computer in front of her. "It looks like Mr. Grub is in room 867. The easiest way to that department is to take the elevator around the corner. Once on the eighth floor, you'll take a left and head down the hall. Once you reach the nurses' station, they'll help you further, as it is a secure department, and you have to be let in."

"Thank you," I tell her, flashing her a smile. She might be the same age as my granny, but she still blushes slightly.

I follow her directions, finding the nurses' station

easily once I make it up to the eighth floor. After talking to the nurse manning the entrance, I'm quickly buzzed in.

"Tyler's parents are expecting you; he still has no idea that you are coming today," the nurse tells me as she escorts me to the correct room.

"Knock-knock," she says, pushing the partially ajar door open so we can walk inside the room. "We have a special visitor here for you today, Tyler," she tells him, moving a privacy curtain out of the way, allowing everyone the ability to see one another.

"Holy shit!" the kid calls out from his hospital bed. "You-you're Lucas Black," he stammers, and I can't hold back the bark of laughter at his cursing.

"Tyler!" I hear his mom scold.

"I am," I confirm to him, closing the distance to the side of his hospital bed. He shifts slightly, sitting up a little taller. I set the bag of things I brought with me down on the foot of his bed before offering him a fist to bump. "Nice to meet you, man," I add.

He looks, shocked and dumbfounded, between me and his parents. I take in the expression on both his mom and dad's faces and see the absolute look of joy in his mom's watery smile.

"Happy birthday, Tyler," she gets out as tears spill down her cheeks.

"Is today your birthday?" I ask. I don't recall that information being relayed to me, but I guess I might have missed it.

"Yep, what a place to turn sixteen," he says, motioning around to the hospital room we are in.

"That's the way it goes sometimes. How much longer until you're done with your treatment?" I ask. I think if I get him talking, it might help him relax more.

"I've got three more rounds of chemo. I'll hopefully get to go home before those are all done. I developed a secondary infection that landed me in here after my last infusion," he explains.

"That sucks." I commiserate with him and he just nods his head in agreement. "You play ball?" I ask, changing the subject.

"Yeah, outfielder, like you," he says.

"Sweet, you hope to go pro?"

"Don't think so, I'm nowhere near good enough."

"None of that, now, you've got to have confidence in your play," I tell him. "It might be hard work, but if you can kick this cancer's as—butt," I say, catching the curse before it is all out and changing up my language, "then you can put in the hard work and follow your dream," I encourage him.

"Yeah, maybe. I've got to make it out of this hospital, first, then high school," he states matter-of-factly. I'm sure fighting for your life in this capacity puts everything into perspective really fast. You learn what is and isn't all that important. Just as you learn who your true friends are in times like these.

I take the rest of my hour visit to talk shop with Tyler and his family, as well as take a handful of pictures with them. He was ecstatic with all the things that Carly sent with me to give him. Ended up being a great birthday present for the kid. He had a smile plastered to his face when it was time for me to head back to the team hotel so I could get in a few hours of rest before the game tonight.

EIGHT

CARMEN

"Holy crap," I murmur, reading over the email for a second time that landed in my in-box a few minutes ago. "He actually can be a stand-up guy."

"Who can be a stand-up guy?" Carly asks, taking a seat in the chair across from my desk.

"The pain in my side," I tell her, knowing that she'll understand exactly who I'm referring to.

"Oh, yeah?" she says, her eyebrows going up. "The hospital trip yesterday?" she asks.

"You knew about that?" I question.

"Yeah, the request came through, I thought you knew we set everything up for it," she says, looking a little nervous.

"Really?" I ask, looking back to my computer screen.

"Yeah, one of the nurses from the hospital called a few days ago, laid out everything and said that the parents were trying to come up with a way to surprise him to lift his spirits. I talked to Lucas before they flew out and he said it wasn't a problem. I even sent a bag of things for him to sign and give the kid," she tells me.

"According to the mom's email, it was his sixteenth birthday," I tell her, glancing back at the email. "She sent a dozen or so images, as well, and said they were already up on Tyler's social media pages and he'd tagged the team's accounts."

"We should retweet them," Carly says, reading my mind.

"You are good," I tell her, pulling out my phone so I can sign in and do just that.

I easily find the post, seeing that it is already gaining quite a lot of comments and shares. Everyone loving the fact that a player would not only go out of his way to go surprise a kid in the hospital, but to also do it while on a road trip. I share the post, tagging Lucas in it, as well, so that he will hopefully also share it.

"I'll send him a text suggesting that he share the posts, as well," Carly states, pulling her own phone out.

"Sure," I say, hopefully hiding the sudden irritation in my voice that came from out of nowhere. Why I'm irritated that one of my employees would be texting one of our players work-related information is a weird thing to be irritated about. But my mind wanders to what else they could be texting about. I shut that thought down before it can take up too much space in my mind.

I finish up sharing the posts to our social media platforms, then set my phone back down on my desk, turning my full attention back to Carly. "What can I do for you?" I ask.

"I actually didn't need anything, I was just coming in to see if you wanted to grab lunch today," she says. I look down at my phone again, seeing that it is, in fact, lunchtime already. This morning was a busy one, apparently.

"I don't, so what did you have in mind?"

"I was thinking of just heading around the corner to the deli for a wrap or salad," she says.

"Sounds good to me," I tell her. I reach into my desk drawer and pull out my wallet. I slip my phone into my back pocket before I follow Carly out of the office.

As soon as we step outside, the heat of the day hits me. The sun feels so good on my skin. I slip my sunglasses off the top of my head and over my eyes to shield them from the brightness. We both must have needed the sun, as we casually walk the block and a half to the little deli where we both end up ordering the daily special, which is a chicken caesar wrap.

"Looks like all their outside seating is full, do you want to head back to the office and sit outside?" I suggest.

"It is scary just how much we think alike." She chuckles. "I was going to suggest the same thing."

We walk back to the office. Our team offices are connected to the large stadium, so we have lots of outside access. We find a table that offers sunshine, but not so much we're blinded by it.

"So," Carly says between bites of her wrap. "Have you given any more thought into a dating app?"

"Ugh." I groan and finish the mouth full of food I have. "Those are the worst," I tell her. "All guys want to do on them is send you dick pics, meet up for a quick fuck, or to catfish you," I explain, pausing long enough to take a quick drink of my lemonade.

"What's wrong?" She quirks an eyebrow. "You don't like looking at random peen? I thought you liked the D?" She smirks.

"Oh, I like me some D, but random pictures of it, no, thank you. That shit isn't pretty."

"You know who probably has a pretty dick?" she says, but more as a statement than a question. "Lucas," she adds before I can answer her, and I almost spit out my lemonade.

"Where did that come from?" I ask her, wiping at my face with a napkin.

"He just has that edge of cockiness to him. Like he knows he's all that and a bag of chips," she says, shrugging her shoulders in a "what are you going to do about it, you know I'm right" kind of gesture.

"He's cocky, that's for sure. And a pain in my ass," I add for good measure.

"I bet he could put something in your ass." She smirks.

"Carly!" I practically screech her name.

"What?" she asks, trying to feign innocence. "You can't tell me you haven't thought for just one second what he'd be like in bed. I'm in a happy committed relationship with a man I love deeply, and *I've* still had a thought or two about what he's packing below the belt and how well he knows how to swing that bat," she says, giving me a pointed look.

"Fine." I roll my eyes at her. "I might have had a thought or two about him. He might have made an appearance or two in my thoughts while in the shower."

"Yeah, he has!" she cheers.

"Okay, that's enough. I have to look him in the eyes and if this conversation keeps going, I won't be able to do that without thinking back to it, or of him naked and doing naughty things."

"If you insist, but maybe you should investigate that a little more. I've seen the way he watches you when you're walking away from him. His eyes never leave your ass," she says, shrugging her shoulders again as she reaches for her own drink.

"Never going to happen. I don't date players."

"Rules are meant to be broken. Plus, isn't that *your* rule and not the team's?" she presses.

"So, what," I tell her. "It isn't like I'm his type, nor is he mine. So there's no reason to put any more thought into the idea. It's never going to happen," I tell her, closing the book on this conversation.

I finish my lunch, wrapping all my trash up and tossing it in one of the large cans not far from the table we're at. I turn around, leaning my back against the table as I close my eyes and soak in the sun.

"I'm headed back inside," Carly says a few minutes later.

I crack my eyes open as she stands. "I'll be following you shortly, I just need a few more minutes here in the sun," I tell her, enjoying the hell out of being able to take this time to just relax.

"Sounds good, I've got some emails to follow up on, so if you need me, you know where to find me," she says before disappearing into the building.

My mind is always turning, always planning multiple things, plus having to be on the ready when something happens with one of the many people associated with the team. From the ownership and management, to the players. I have to deal with media relations for all of them at one point or another. Just like some I deal with more than others. My job is never boring, that's for sure. As hectic and stressful as it can be at times, I wouldn't change it for anything. I love what I do. I love working for the Lightning. It is a great organization to work for, and I'm very lucky to have landed this dream job when I did.

My phone buzzes on the table behind me, so I'm forced to end my time soaking in the sun. When I look at the screen, my eyes instantly roll as I see who's calling me.

"Carmen Gibson," I answer the call. My voice is laced with so much fakeness, I could almost puke from all of it.

"Carmen," the caller greets. "This is Bella King from TMZ," she tells me, and launches into why she's calling before I can interject. "I'm calling to get a statement on the situation from earlier today."

I'm a little surprised, as TMZ usually only cares about gossip that I'm trying to keep as quiet as possible, not the news that we actually want picked up and spread like gospel. I will never assume with someone like this, as they'll sometimes try and trick unsuspecting people into giving up a morsel of information that wasn't previously released.

"I'll need a little bit more information before I can provide a statement, can you tell me whom, exactly, you're calling about and what situation you're referring to?"

I swear I can hear gum popping on the other end of the line, which just goes to show you the level of professionalism. "I'm calling in reference to Lucas Black," she says, the annoyance obvious, at this point.

"A request came in last week from a children's hospital in Florida," I start to tell her the details.

"Actually," she interjects, "I'm calling regarding the other announcement about Lucas," she states and I'm sure I lose all my color as my mind starts reeling as to what other announcement she's talking about.

"For any comments on anything not related to the team, please reach out to Mr. Black's manager or personal PR company." I give her my nicest blow off and end the call, basically hanging up on her. I type his name into my Google search as I haul ass back to my office.

"Carly!" I call out as I pass by her office as I run to my own. She must hear the panic in my voice as she comes running into my office.

"What's wrong?"

"I have no idea, TMZ just called asking for a comment on the 'situation' with Lucas. I thought it was a little weird because usually hospital visits aren't their thing, but I went with it. When I started to give them a response about how the hospital visit was set up, she interrupted me and said she was calling about the other 'situation'." I pause long enough to wake my computer up and type Lucas's name into a Google search. The screen immediately loads and is flooded with articles that have hit within the last thirty minutes.

A Secret Baby for Baseball's Newest Hotshot?

I read the headlines one after another. "Well, looks like he knocked up a stripper," I tell Carly.

"You've got to be kidding me?" she says as she plops down in the chair across from my desk. "That man needs to learn how to keep it in his pants."

"And wrap it up." I grimace. I don't need to be thinking about him and his junk and whether he wraps it up when he's having sex. Especially with a stripper.

"Do you want me to reach out to him, see if he's got his PR firm on this? If he's smart, he'll demand a paternity test just to make sure she's not trying to use him for money or fame. You know she wouldn't be the first, and most definitely won't be the last to do that."

I glance at the clock, checking the time, then checking the itinerary for the team. Since they're still on the road, I have an hour-by-hour breakdown of where they'll be when. "He should be at the hotel," I tell her, hitting the speaker button on my phone before I dial his number.

It rings four times before flipping over to his generic voice mail. At the end of the beep, I do my best to control myself as I leave him a quick message. "Lucas, Carmen here, I need to talk to you about this current baby situation. I'm fielding calls from TMZ. I need to know if you have your own PR firm on this or if we need to coordinate things. If no one else has advised you of this, yet, I'd highly recommend you request a paternity test ASAP. Many women will lie about a baby on the way or whose it is, when a professional athlete is in the equation. Just be careful, and please call me back ASAP."

I hang up the call before I start ranting, especially since it is just a voice mail box and not actually Lucas.

"What do you want to do?" Carly asks, her voice soft and reserved.

"Until we know if his PR firm is already on this, we can work on drafting up a statement, but need to hold off on actually submitting it to anyone. I don't want to overstep."

NINE

LUCAS

I'm sitting at a table with some of my teammates in the back of the hotel's bar. We've just finished our lunch and are shooting the shit, when my phone starts buzzing constantly on the table. I turn it over to see the screen blowing up with notifications. When that happens, it is never a good sign, so I quickly grab it, swiping up to check out what is going on today.

"Shit, son," JJ says from across the table. "Looks like someone got himself a little bit of drama going on." He smirks.

"Asshole," I call him, glaring at him over the top of my phone. My glare must not be all that intimidating to him, as he just smiles back like he knows something I don't.

I skim the posts, one on Twitter, specifically, catches my eye and has now been shared over a thousand times in the few minutes it has been posted. Some chick, one I don't even recognize, has tagged me and is claiming I'm the father of her unborn child.

"Just take a deep breath and get Carmen on the phone," Derek says, slapping a hand on my shoulder as I do my best to pull oxygen into my lungs and not pass out because I'm freaking out inside. I know down in my soul that this girl is lying. All she sees with me is a big fat paycheck if she claims I'm her baby daddy.

"I'll call my own, first," I grunt out as I pull up my contacts list. Before I can hit the button, my phone starts ringing, and it is Brent, my agent calling.

"Lucas." Brent's deep voice comes through the line. "Talk to me, kid."

"She's lying," I blurt out.

"Okay, and what makes you so confident about that?" he questions.

"First off, I don't recognize her at all from the little I was able to see on her profile. Plus, I *always* use protection."

"Protection isn't one-hundred percent, you should know that," he shoots back.

"I know, but I just have a feeling about this one," I tell him.

"I've already shot a message off to PR, asking them to get on this ASAP. For now, no comments to any media. You got that?" he asks.

"Loud and clear."

"We'll make a announcement in the next hour, basically stating that a paternity test will be requested to determine if you are, in fact, the father, and if that proves you are then you will step up and provide for the baby and reasonable support for his or her mother. We'll also request that the media leave you alone on this matter, as you are still processing the news, seeing as how the young woman took to Twitter to inform you of this potential child."

"I can live with all of that," I tell him. My phone starts buzzing in my ear, thanks to an incoming call. I pull it away, just to check to see who is calling. Carmen's contact pops up, but I let her go to voice mail, knowing that she's probably calling to rip me a new one due to this newest drama. I swear, I can't win when it comes to keeping my name out of the spotlight. She's never going to think better of me if shit like this keeps popping up.

I STEP OUT OF THE SHOWER, WRAPPING A TOWEL around my waist. After the bombshell dropped this afternoon, I played like shit tonight. Dropped a ball I should have never dropped, which allowed Tampa to score a run, then struck out every time I was up to bat.

I get dressed as quickly as I can, not really socializing with any of the guys. I'm in a shitty mood, between today's drama, the shitty way I played, the loss of the game. It all is just weighing down on me tonight. I just need a night to escape everything, and plan to do just that when I get back to the hotel.

Just as I'm entering my hotel room, my phone starts

buzzing in my pocket. I pull it out, seeing my sister's smiling face lighting up the screen. Seeing how late it is, I worry something might be wrong with my nephew, so I answer the call as quickly as I can.

"Everything okay with Milo?" I ask as her face fills the screen.

"Oh, yeah, he's fine. I was worried about you. How are you holding up?" she asks.

"It's been one hell of a day, but I'll survive," I tell her, dropping to sit on the edge of the bed.

"I saw the press release, how are you really handling the news?" she presses. My sister is one of my very best friends. We are only thirteen months apart, and while that contributed to us fighting like cats and dogs growing up, we're now closer than ever. I'd do anything for her, my nephew, Milo, or my brother-in-law, Brad.

"She's so full of shit, Tiff. I've never slept with that girl, let alone gotten her pregnant. I'm hopeful that we can do the DNA test as soon as I get back to Indianapolis, but I'm not sure how all that works, since the baby isn't born yet. It is going to really suck if I have to wait until it is born to find out."

"Depending on how far along she is, they can do a simple blood test from what I was researching earlier. It is ninety-nine percent accurate. They can also do an amniocentesis, but that is more invasive and comes with some risks."

"I'd be fine with the blood test if it is that accurate," I tell her.

"That's what I'd suggest starting with. The lab that I

found looks like they offer same day rush results for another five-hundred bucks, otherwise, it can take three to five days."

"Five-hundred bucks will be well worth the cost, just to know for sure within a day," I tell her and mean every word. I'd rather drop a couple grand on this test and know for sure than to spend only a few hundred and have it hanging over my head. "I think a lawyer has to step in and get involved. Brent was going to handle everything for me and let me know once I'm back in town."

"When do you fly in?" Tiffany questions.

"After tomorrow's game."

"So, you could potentially be getting the test done in as soon as two days from now."

"I guess so, but that also means they have to get this chick to agree to it by then."

"Do you even know her name?" Tiff asks.

"Nope, do you?" I ask her as I push back on the bed, leaning against the headboard as I get a little comfortable.

"The report said Abigail."

"Yeah, no recollection of an Abigail, ever."

"Do you need to check your little black book?" She chuckles, giving me shit.

"Don't be a bitch."

"Me? A bitch to my little brother, the hotshot of major league baseball?" she asks all innocent like. "Never!" She breaks out into a maniacal laugh and I can't help but smirk at her antics. "That's the smile I was looking for." She beams. "I knew I could make you laugh at this crazy situation."

"Thanks, Tiff. I knew if anyone could get me through all this BS, it would be you. Now, how's my nephew today?"

"He's good, really good, actually."

"The cast giving him any problems?"

"He's finally getting used to it, I think. Although, it is still like a little weapon attached to his leg. I've got some nasty bruises to show from the times he's accidently hit me with it."

"Damn, well, only a few more weeks and he can get it taken off."

"I'm so ready for that day. He's starting to stink since we can't give him a full shower or bath."

"No worse than my gym bag growing up."

"Gah, don't remind me. That thing was vile."

"Well, I should get off to bed, it's been a long day. I'll call you once I'm back in town. Love you, Tiff."

"Love you, too, bro. Hang in there and we'll get you past all of this. Once it all blows over, maybe it is time for you to find someone to settle down with, leave your manwhore ways behind you."

"Yeah, yeah. There is one woman who I wouldn't mind pursuing," I let slip, and know I've made a big mistake.

"Wait, hold up. What did you just say?" Tiffany says, sitting up and giving me a WTF look via the camera.

"There might be one woman who drives me insane —the good kind of insane–but I don't think she likes me all that much, so I'm sure it isn't going to happen," I tell her.

"And who is this mysterious woman that has piqued your interest?"

"Carmen Gibson, she's the team's PR manager."

"Tell me more. A workplace romance, and the one person who has to deal with all your fuckups. I love this."

"Yeah, well, she doesn't usually like me all that much, so I don't see how I'd ever convince her to go out with me or give me a chance. She sees me as nothing more than a player man-child."

"Well, little brother, maybe it is time that you show her you are a man and have given up your childish manwhore ways."

"This whole baby thing isn't helping that image at all. And to think, I was doing good. I haven't been with a woman since the strip club incident."

"Well, give it a few days, maybe a few more weeks. Let all the chips fall as they're going to fall and then move forward. Even if this Abigail chick is telling the truth and the baby is yours, it isn't like you'd be the first guy to have a baby with a stranger. It is what you do to step up and take care of the baby that shows your true character. You know I love you, but I'm here to tell you, little brother, that sometimes you get in your own way. Just lay low, and I'll be right by your side as things unfold."

"Thanks, Tiff. I love you. Give Milo a kiss from Uncle Lucas."

"He's sleeping, but I'll do so in the morning. Maybe on your next day off you can come over for the day. He'd love to have a day to hang with his favorite uncle."

"Damn straight he would," I tell her before we say our last goodbyes and end the call.

THANKS TO MY MANAGER AND ATTORNEY, A NURSE IS coming to the stadium today to draw my blood for the paternity test. Abigail agreed to the test, eventually. Tried to swindle money out of me to do it now, but the threat of a lawsuit had a way of convincing her that she needed to agree to this, and now. Everyone agreed that she could also show up here at the facility so the same nurse could draw her blood, as well, to take it straight to the lab to be processed. I paid the extra money to have the results rushed to us by the end of the day.

"Just a small poke," the older lady tells me after wiping my arm down with an alcohol wipe. She pushes the needle into my arm, and the tube immediately starts filling with my blood. Since they're only running the one test, she only needs the one small vial of blood. "Apply some pressure here for me," she says after pressing a cotton ball over the needle before pulling it out of my arm. After shaking the tube with my blood back and forth a couple times, she places the label on it, then drops it into the bio-hazard bag. She offers me some medical tape to hold the gauze in place, now that my arm has stopped bleeding.

"Thanks, now I'll have the results by close of business today?" I ask her.

"Yes, you should have them by five p.m. If you don't,

then, call the office. We're open until eight, so it is possible they'll go out after five, but we do our best to get same-day rush orders out by five."

"Thanks," I tell her, rubbing my palms along my pants. They're damp from sweat as I worry about the outcome from this test.

I watch from a window as the nurse takes Abigail's blood. I didn't really want to see or talk to her today but watching with my own two eyes the blood being drawn helps calm my anxiety that she'd somehow tamper with the test to make it come out with fake results. I don't know why I'm so convinced that she's trying to trap me. Probably because since she made the announcement and my attorney contacted her, it was all about the money to her, added to the fact that I don't remember this girl from anywhere.

With the blood draws done, I head for the gym. I need to do some heavy lifting or something to get my mind off watching the minutes tick by on the clock.

"How many more miles are you going?" JJ asks, jumping on the treadmill next to mine.

"Until my legs can't go any farther," I pant out between breaths. I look down and see that I've already put in about five miles. "Maybe another three or four?" I toss out.

"Any word yet?" he asks. The guys all knew what was going down today, and therefore have given me a wide birth as I await the results.

"Nope, still waiting," I tell him. I hit the button and the belt slows me down, bringing me to a stop. I gulp down my bottle of Gatorade, then follow that up with a full bottle of water. With as much as I've sweated out today, I need all the hydration I can get.

"Just don't kill yourself, in the meantime. No number of squats or miles run are going to make the results come in faster or change them."

"Just trying to keep my mind focused on something other than the email that hasn't arrived and the time on the clock," I tell him honestly.

"Man, I know what it's like to be waiting on that test. I've done it myself not that long ago. Yes, my situation was a little bit different, as the baby was already born and was in my care, but I still needed to know for sure that she was mine. The lab I used didn't offer a same day rush option, so I had to wait a few days. They were the longest days of my life. Seriously, they were. When the results came in, I was almost too scared to open them. By that point, I didn't want them to say that Evie wasn't mine. I had already fallen in love with her by then, and in my heart, it didn't really matter what a piece of paper said, I knew she was mine. She looked way too much like me to be anyone else's kid."

"I'm actually relieved that the kid isn't born yet. I'd feel bad, I think, if it was, and I was here denying it was mine," I tell him.

"If the test comes back and you are the dad, what are you going to do?" he asks.

"Whatever I have to do to provide for it."

"And that proves that you're a good man," he tells me

before putting his earbuds into his ears and turning up the speed on his treadmill.

Since slowing down, my legs have now turned to Jell-O, so I guess it is time to get off this treadmill and move on to something else.

I slip my own earbuds back in as I exit the gym and head for the locker room. I strip down to my boxers once in the locker room and sink into one of the ice baths that are always ready for us to use. The immediate sting of the cold water has my body shriveling up, trying to protect itself from the freezing cold water. It takes a minute or so before my body starts to relax, and the cold goes to work helping my muscles recover from the beating I put them through today in the gym. I don't normally go that hard on gym days, but the situation at hand kind of dictated that.

"Everyone decent?" Coach's voice calls out into the locker room. That usually means that a female is about to enter the room. Since you can get quite the eye full in this room at any given time, we make a ritual of checking before any females are allowed in.

"I'm in the ice bath in my boxers," I call out, letting him know I'm in here.

"Do you have a towel?" he asks, poking his head into the area that our ice baths are in.

"Over there," I tell him, pointing at one on the bench.

"How much longer until you're out? Carmen needs to talk to you."

"I can hop out now, take a quick shower, and then head up to her office, if that would be easier," I tell him, not really liking the idea, but knowing that I can't get out of talking to her today.

"I'll let her know. Now, don't waste her time, get a hop on it," Coach calls over his shoulder as he makes his way back to the door. I do as I'm told and hop out of the ice bath. Instead of standing under the hot spray, letting it warm up my cold body, I quickly wash up, then get out and dressed. Fifteen minutes later, I'm walking through the halls of the team building toward Carmen's office when my phone dings with a new email.

I stop in the doorway to her office, scanning over the subject line and sender information. My blood pressure rises as I see that it is the email I've been waiting for since my blood was drawn at eight this morning.

"What's wrong?" she asks, coming to my side. She must be able to tell that something is going on from my stance.

"I just got the email," I tell her, turning my phone so she can read what is showing on my screen.

"Oh!" she says, a little shocked. "How about you come in and sit down, then open it."

I do as she suggests, taking a seat on the small couch in her office rather than one of the chairs across from her desk.

I turn the phone in the palms of my hands, not yet ready to read the results.

"Lucas," she says, her voice warm and calming. I've never heard it like that, and it squeezes around my heart. She sits down on the couch next to me, placing her hand over my own. "Whatever the email says, you'll be fine and will get through it."

"She's lying," I tell her, looking straight into her eyes. I don't know why I want her to believe me so bad, but I do. I want her to believe me so that maybe, just maybe, I can convince her to go out on a date with me. Convince her I'm not as bad as the media likes to portray me as. Make her see those few times she's had to clean up my image were the minority and not my normal. Just a few stupid decisions I made in the past year.

"Do you want me to read it first?" she offers.

"Yes," I tell her. I fumble with my phone, turning it around and swiping it open. I hand it over then grab her hand back, linking our fingers together. "Maybe read it to yourself, then tell me," I suggest, gripping her fingers a little tighter.

"Sure," she says. I watch as she taps the screen of my phone, opening the email up. It feels like an entire day lapse before she looks up at me. A small smile starts tugging at the corner of her mouth and I want to devour it.

"I'm ready," I croak out, finding her eyes with my own and not letting that connection go.

"With an accuracy of ninety-nine percent, you are not the father," she says and her smile now fills her face.

"Fuck yes!" I blurt out and pull her into my arms. My lips are against hers before I even know what the hell I'm doing, and I don't even see the hand coming until it connects with my cheek. The sting of the slap has me pulling back and sucking in air like I just ran a marathon at a six-minute mile the entire way.

"What the ever-loving-fuck, Lucas?" Carmen screeches, her fingers covering her kiss-swollen lips.

"Shit," I mumble. "I'm sorry. It just happened. I was shocked and happy over the results," I tell her and hope that she'll accept my apology.

"You can't just go kissing women without their permission. I could have you written up for sexual harassment."

"I said I'm sorry." I take my hat off, running my fingers through my hair in my frustration. "It won't happen again."

"Damn straight it won't," she says, standing from the couch. She hands me my phone back before walking to the other side of her office and behind her desk. I watch every move she makes as she pulls her chair out and takes a seat. "Would you like me to put out any press releases or do you want to leave that up to your lawyer and manager?" she asks, turning right back to business.

"I'll let Brent handle it," I tell her. I tap on my phone, bringing up Brent's contact and hitting the call button.

"Lucas, any word, yet?" he asks.

"Yep, the email came in just a few minutes ago. Just like I've been claiming since the beginning, I'm not the father."

"Told you the truth would prevail, kid," he says, and it grits on my nerves every time he refers to me as kid. I know the man has been in the athlete management business for a long time, maybe even longer than I've been alive, but I'm still no fucking kid. I'm a twenty-four-year-old man who makes millions of dollars a year.

"I knew it would. Just tell me what you need from me and let's make all of this headache go away," I tell him.

"Will do, Lucas. We might consider agreeing to a short interview in a week or two. Give your side of the story and explain what you went through, being thrown under the bus, all thanks to someone else lie and attempt at a money grab."

"I don't know about that. Won't that just keep her in the spotlight longer, and this at the front of people's minds?" I question.

"Possibly, but think about it, as it can be a good way to get your side of the story out. Let people hear directly from you what it was like stressing over this news and waiting for the results. Let them know that you would have stepped up and done the right thing had the results been different. We can discuss it more after you've had a chance to think it over."

"Okay," I agree before we disconnect the call, even though I already know that I have no intentions of sitting down for an interview about this mess.

I stand from the couch, taking in the sight before me. Carmen's lips are still a little swollen, and fuck does that make me want to kiss them again. "Thanks for helping me, and I'm sorry again about the kiss."

"Anytime, Lucas. I'm not here to be a pain in your ass, even if you are a pain in mine." She smiles up at me and fuck, there goes my cock.

"I'll work on not being a pain in your ass going

forward, how does that sound?" I suggest as a peace offering.

"Like the best news I've heard all day." She laughs. "Now, go on, celebrate, responsibly," she adds as an afterthought.

"Thanks," I tell her before exiting her office.

TEN

CARMEN

I BOARD THE TEAM JET; WE'RE HEADED TO OUR FIRST playoff series against Toronto. I don't often go with the team on trips, but there is a lot that happens around the post-season, so I get to travel with the team for these series.

I take a seat about five or so rows back from the front. From past experience, I know the guys like to spread out in the back of the jet, some sleep, some play games, or watch movies. I've got some emails to catch up on, and thanks to the on-board Wi-Fi, I plan to work the entire flight.

"Is this seat taken?" A deep voice interrupts my attention on my computer screen. I look up to see Lucas standing in the aisle, waiting for my answer.

"I don't think so," I tell him and he slides into the row, taking the seat next to me.

"What are you working on?" he questions, trying to look at my laptop screen.

"Just work emails," I tell him, closing the lid to my computer and turning slightly to face him better. "What can I help you with?"

"Nothing specific, I just thought we could get to know one another better. We didn't get off on the best foot when I arrived, and I wanted to fix that, now that I haven't been a 'pain in your ass' as you called me a few weeks ago," he says, using air quotes around my words.

"You have done much better staying out of trouble, although, I've got my eye on you," I warn him.

"Baby, you can keep those beautiful blues on me whenever you like," he says, winking at me.

"Your one liners won't work on me," I tell him, batting my eyelashes at him.

"You wound me," he says, clutching at his heart.

"I don't think your ego knows what it's like to be turned down by a real woman," I state.

"I've been shot down plenty of times. I wasn't always this good looking. Hell, back in my high school days, I was the jock who looked more like one of the computer nerds. It took me awhile to grow into my sexiness," he tells me, running a palm down his torso—his very fit and chiseled torso—that I've maybe seen a time or two when he's had his shirt off. The same one I've got a mental image of that might get pulled up when I'm alone in my bed with a vibrator, or in the shower.

"I can't even picture you as the geeky kid. I'd have assumed you were always the kid with all the swagger and charm."

"Oh, I had charm." He laughs, shaking his head.

"Well, at least, *I* thought I had charm and game, when in reality I was so far from cool it isn't even funny. But after my senior year, I found a love for the weight room and started working out more. I started paying attention to what I was putting into my body and the effect it had on my game. How eating too much of one thing might slow me down the next day."

"That's great that you were able to figure it out so early. Most guys don't even start to pay attention to that until later in their careers."

"I realized around that time that if I really wanted to take playing seriously; I needed to be serious about it and everything that could potentially affect my ability to play professional. I wasn't lucky enough to have colleges recruiting me or offering me scholarships. I played my first two seasons at a community college, while working part-time and busting my ass off to keep my grades up so I was eligible to play. Once I finished my associate degree, I was able to get a walk-on spot at a larger state university, but that still didn't come with scholarship money right away. My coach pulled some strings mid-season and got me a partial scholarship. I think that was more so that I wasn't almost passing out on the field because I was tired all the time from working so many hours on top of studying, working out and, of course, practice and games. Once that scholarship was awarded, I didn't have to work so many hours in order to afford to go to school."

"I don't think any of that is a bad thing. It taught you that if you work hard, put in the effort, that you can achieve your dreams. You just have to want it bad enough and you can make it happen."

"Yep," he says, popping the p. The flight attendant stops at our row, right then, so our attention is pulled from one another to her.

"Can I get either of you something to drink before takeoff?" she asks.

"Do you have hot tea?" I ask.

"We do." She smiles at me.

"I'll take that with some honey, if you have any."

"We should," she confirms. "And for you, Mr. Black?" she asks Lucas.

"Just a water, please," he asks politely.

"Right away," she says, heading back for her prep area. She returns a few minutes later with a large cup with piping hot water in it, along with a small basket of assorted teas and the tiniest little bottle of honey that I've ever seen. It is so little and cute; I can't get enough of it. It reminds me of getting the mini ketchup bottles when you order room service at a fancy hotel.

"Do you get to travel with the team often?" Lucas asks once we're in the air.

"Playoffs are usually the only time I go, unless we've got a special event going on over a road trip. Otherwise, I just do my job from the office," I tell him.

"What made you want to work for an MLB team?" he inquires.

"I interned for the Lightning when I was still in college. I loved the atmosphere, and all that came with working for a professional sports team, that when they offered me a job after I graduated, I jumped at the opportunity. I've been with them for the last six years already and was promoted to my current position about a year and a half ago, when the former manager left for another company."

"So, like me, your hard work paid off," he muses.

"I guess you could look at it like that. Those first few weeks as an intern were brutal. I didn't know anything—*anything*—about baseball. I'd probably been to two, maybe three games in my entire life before getting the job, so I had a large learning curve when it came to the game, and hell, I still don't know everything there is to know about the sport."

"That's pretty funny, the girl that knows nothing about the sport gets an important job within a sports organization."

"My friends and family were all a little shocked. My brother, although not a huge baseball fan, is still a bit jealous, if I'm being honest," I tell him. I don't know why it all of a sudden feels natural to open up and talk to Lucas. Maybe because he's the one that initiated this conversation and has opened up to me some already.

"What does he do?" he asks.

"He's in the Army, has been for around twelve years already. Went in straight out of high school."

"Cool, do you have other siblings?"

"Nope, just my bother. He's married to his high school sweetheart, Heather, and they have my nephew, Simon. What about you, you've got any siblings?"

"I do, my sister, Tiffany, is basically my best friend.

She's married to my brother-in-law, Brad, and they also have a little boy, Milo, who is about three."

"Oh, that sounds like a fun age. My nephew is about nine months old, so still is a little on the innocent side."

"Milo is a fun little kid. He's an uncle's boy, that's for sure. If I'm around, he won't listen to anyone but me. It drives my sister and brother-in-law crazy. He'll sometimes cry for me, which breaks my heart when it happens and we aren't in town or I can't go to him."

"Oh, they live in Indianapolis?" I ask, a little shocked that he has local family. "I didn't think you were from around here," I tell him.

"I'm not but it's been fate, I guess. Brad was offered a job in Indianapolis shortly after he graduated with his MBA, so they packed up and moved here. Then, when I was drafted, it felt like fate was at it again, and again when I was called up to actually play for the big team and not in the minors."

"Definitely sounds like a lot of fate working in your favor."

"It really was."

"Does your sister work, or does she get to stay home with Milo?"

"She's home with Milo," he tells me, but the way he says it, I can tell he's holding something back.

"That's great! Have they made it to any of the games?"

"A couple, but the evening ones make it a late night for Milo, and they are a bit long for his attention span."

"I can understand that." I chuckle. "They're some-times long for me."

"Blasphemy," he says dramatically. "So, what do you like to do outside of work?"

"I sometimes forget what it's like to have a life outside of work. When I'm not putting out fires from Friday night shenanigans," I tell him, giving him a pointed look, "I like to start my weekend off with some yoga. Other than that, the normal things, reading, hanging out with friends and family, traveling."

"What is number one on your wish list of places to visit next?" he asks.

"Well, that depends on what the trip is for. If I'm looking for an exploration type trip, I'd love to go down to Peru and hike my way around for a week or two, or maybe down to Africa and go out on a safari or go to one of the giraffe sanctuaries. If it's a relaxation trip, maybe with a lover, then somewhere that we can just lay out on the beach and be in the water. Book a bungalow that's out over the water, like in Bora Bora. I'd also love to make it up to Alaska at some point and spend a few weeks just exploring."

"I take it you don't get to travel as much as you'd like to?" he asks, breaking into my thoughts.

"No, I don't like to take time off during the season, as that is when I'm busiest. That leaves the off season, and well, that doesn't leave me with all that much time, and some of the places I'd like to visit need to be visited during the summertime. So, until I either decide that it is okay to take off time during the season, or move on to a different job, I'll stick to traveling during the off season."

"I can see how that would be limiting."

We fall into a bit of comfortable silence, long enough that I open my laptop back up and take care of a handful of emails. Most are simple things I'm able to easily answer.

I sneak a few peeks at Lucas while I work. He's slipped in his AirPods and has closed his eyes as he leans back in his seat. The man sitting next to me is nothing like the one that showed up a few months ago. He's like an onion. Has multiple layers and once you peel them back, you realize that he's not so bad.

ELEVEN

LUCAS

I sit in the hotel bar, the feeling a little déjà vu-ish, however, this time, I'm not worried about getting a call that someone has dropped a bomb and used my name in the mix. The biggest difference, this time, is the fact that Carmen is sitting right next to me. Because we're in a large booth, her leg is next to my own and as people move about, we occasionally touch. The control it is taking to keep from reaching down and caressing her leg is strong right now.

I watch her as best as I can from the corner of my eye, and use talking to JJ, who's on the other side of her, as a good excuse to almost always be looking that direction. I watch as she takes sips of her glass of wine. It isn't lost on me that she's been nursing the same glass the entire time we've been down here.

"You don't have to hoard your wine, I'm sure they can bring you another glass," I tease her as she takes yet another small sip.

"Aren't you just full of jokes." She smirks at me. "I've limited myself to just one glass, I don't need to wake up with a wine headache tomorrow, plus, I'd like to make it back to my room in one piece."

"I'll make sure you make it back in one piece," I tell her as my eyes scan the parts of her body that I can easily see with the table in my way. I press my knee against her and don't miss the way her breath hiccups and her skin turns that fucking shade of red I love so much at my touch.

My dick presses against the zipper of my slacks the rest of the time we're in this damn booth. Carmen doesn't move her knee from pressing against mine, so I don't move, either. If anything, we move closer to one another. She's like a magnetic force and I'm drawn to her.

As some of the other guys start heading toward their rooms for the night, Carmen takes the opportunity to slip from the booth, as well, so I follow her out. "Thanks for letting me crash your evening, boys, but it's time for me to turn in before I turn into a pumpkin," she jokes.

"Of course, you're welcome to join us whenever," Matt O'Riley tells her.

"I'll walk you back to your room," I say only loud enough that Carmen can hear me. "This hotel might have tight security because we're staying here, but that won't stop some creep from following you."

"Thank you," she says, biting at her bottom lip. I didn't think that it was possible, but my cock swells a little more. At this point, I'm sure I'll have an imprint of my zipper for days to come.

I drop a hand to Carmen's lower back as we walk through the lobby of the hotel and onto a waiting elevator. The entire team is on the twenty-second floor, which requires a key card to get to. Carmen slides her card into the slit before hitting the button. I don't know if she realizes, but she leans back into my touch. The press of her against me has me wishing I could feel a whole lot more of her body pressed against my own, preferably with less clothing between us.

The elevator ride is quick, and before I know it, we're exiting and heading down the long hall. She comes to a stop outside room twenty-two-twenty-two. "This is me, thanks for making sure I got back safely."

I take a step closer, reaching out and tucking a strand of her hair behind her ear. My fingers caress her soft skin, and that feeling from a few minutes ago is back and stronger than ever. I watch her eyes as my fingers caress her skin, she isn't pushing me away, which I'm taking as a win. I take another step closer, she's now backed up against her door and I'm mere inches from her. "I'm going to kiss you now, unless you tell me not to," I whisper, giving her a few seconds to process my words. When she doesn't protest, my lips cover hers as I pull her in until we're flush against one another.

My senses are on overload. I can feel her hardened nipples through the thin T-shirt she's wearing. She not only lets me deepen the kiss, but she also pushes up onto her toes, giving me better access to her mouth.

I break the kiss; we are in the hallway, after all, and

could get busted at any moment. I rest my forehead against hers and love the shade of red she's turned for me.

"Red." I smirk and trace the pad of my pointer finger from her cheek to the V between her breasts that are on display. She doesn't slap me away, so that's a positive.

"Did you want to come in?" she asks. Her question catches me off guard as it was the last thing I expected to come from her lips. To be honest, I was half expecting another slap across the face once she came to her senses and realized that we just made out in the hallway of a hotel.

"Lead the way," I tell her, my voice a little grittier than it usually is. She turns around, sliding the key along the sensor until we hear the lock disengage. She turns the handle, opening the door into her suite. She shocks me once again when she reaches out, grabbing me by the belt and pulling me along after her. The door slams shut behind me and my resolve snaps right along with the click of the door. I grab her, pulling her into me as I reach down and pick her up off the floor. My hands cup her ass cheeks as she wraps her legs around my torso. Her ass in my hands has me almost coming in my jeans.

I press her against the wall, our lips finding one another, yet again, as we both start to tear at each another's clothes in a race to find skin-on-skin contact. I pull back, breaking our kiss, but only long enough to pull her shirt off over her head. Her tits are the most perfect set I've laid my eyes and hands on, and that's saying something. I cup them, rubbing my thumbs over her nipples.

The friction the lace of her bra adds causes them to pucker even more under my touch.

I lift her a little higher and drop my mouth to her breasts, and I kiss across the full mounds that spill from the tops of the cups of her bra. I dip my tongue beneath the lace, flicking her nipple with the tip. I can feel the moan that falls from her lips as it starts deep inside her core. I move to her other breast, repeating my movements yet again. I love the scrape of her nails as she runs her fingers through my hair, holding on as I worship her body.

Lowering her down my body slightly, I grind my hard cock into her center as I take her lips once again. I swallow her moans as she grinds against me, searching for her own release.

"That's it, baby," I whisper against her lips.

"More," she moans, then sucks my bottom lip between her teeth.

I wrap my arms around her again, anchoring her to me as I pull away from the wall. I look over her shoulder and into the suite to find the bed. I need her naked and now. I walk deeper into the room and through a door, finding the king-size bed in the center. I close the distance, setting her down on the edge.

"Tell me now if this isn't what you want," I state, giving her an out before we get any farther. My balls might kill me if I have to walk out of this room right now, but I'd do it.

Instead of words, Carmen looks up at me, desire practically dripping from her eyes as she reaches once again for my belt. She unbuckles it, never breaking eye contact as she does. The slide of my zipper moving down and allowing my cock a little extra room now that it's not pressed up against the metal. Before I even realize what's happening, Carmen has my jeans and boxer briefs off my hips and halfway down my thighs. She's wrapped her hand around my hard shaft and is stroking it. I can't take my eyes off my cock in her hand and watch as she wraps her lips around my crown.

"Fuuuuck," I groan as she takes me deeper into her mouth. I hold back the urge to thrust my hips and deep throat her. I let her set the pace as I gather her hair in my hand, fisting it at the back of her head so that it's out of the way.

The way her tongue teases me as it runs up and down with each bob of her head has me almost coming down her throat. I tap her cheek, warning her that I'm close to coming, but she doesn't stop. If anything, she doubles down, reaching between my legs and fondling my balls and rubbing a finger against the sensitive skin between my ass and ball sac. Between all the sensations, I can't hold back my orgasm any longer and come down her throat.

I'd never have guessed, even a day ago, that Carmen was a swallower, but she is. Every last fucking drop I give her, she takes. With my cock still twitching, I pull from her mouth, then push her back on the bed. "My turn." I give her a devilish look, one that I'm sure tells her just how hungry I am to taste her. She shimmies back on the mattress until she's splayed out in the center of it. I reach up and do as she did to me, unbuttoning and removing her jeans and panties from her body. I slip a hand behind her back, unclipping her bra and tossing that into the same pile her jeans and panties are in.

I look down at the gorgeous woman splayed out and on display for my viewing pleasure only. I could get used to looking at her and only her. "So beautiful," I murmur as I hover over her. I bring my lips to her neck, sucking and kissing as I slowly make my way down her body. I do my best to cover every inch I can reach as I slide down her body until my mouth is level with her pussy. I place a kiss against her mound and run two fingers through her folds. I find them swollen, wet and ready for me.

Carmen's inner thighs quiver as I place a kiss to each of them before my mouth devours her clit. I flick it with the tip of my tongue before sucking it hard into my mouth. Her body trembles, back arching as I slip two fingers inside her wet pussy. I quickly find her most tender spots and follow the clues her body is giving me with every flick of my fingertips and tongue. It doesn't take long and her thighs are clenching tightly around my head, as her screams of pleasure tumble from her lips as she falls over the edge of ecstasy.

Once her body has stopped pulsing around my fingers, I pull them from her and lap one last time at her very sensitive clit. Her body trembles when my tongue makes contact, and I can't help but chuckle against her skin. "So responsive," I murmur.

Pushing up the bed, I lay down next to her. We're both relaxed and sated after our mutual orgasms. I let her bask in the hormones that are no doubt coursing through her veins right now, giving her a little bit before I press on to anything else that might transpire tonight. I just had the most gorgeous woman's clit in my mouth, her taste still prominent on my tongue. There's no way I want to rush her, at this point, and ruin my chances of actually sinking balls deep inside of her body. Letting her ruin me for good.

"Come here," I say, my words coming out just above a whisper. I lift up my arm, giving her the perfect place to curl her body into. I can't stop the smile from filling my face when she rolls into my side, tucking her body against my own. She finally settles once her head is resting on my chest, a leg placed overtop my own and her hand resting on my abs.

"This okay?" she asks. I can't tell if she's tired or if that is worry in her voice that I'm not okay with this.

"It's perfect," I tell her, wrapping my arm around her body, loving the feel of her skin against mine.

We lay here in silence. I can't see her face, so I'm not sure if she's fallen asleep. I know I could easily fall asleep like this with Carmen in my arms. I realize she isn't sleeping when her fingers start tracing the ink I have along my ribs. A large compass, always leading me back home when I need it the most. When I start to make bad decisions and need that pull to get my head on straight.

"You okay?" I finally break the silence to ask.

"Perfect," she whispers into my skin. I feel her lips brush against my chest as she turns her head slightly. My cock stirs at the contact of her lips and any spot on my body. I roll us until she's under me and I can hover over her once again.

"I can show you perfect," I say as my lips find the soft skin just below her ear. She shifts, allowing our bodies to be a little better aligned, and I can feel her wetness as I slide my once again hard cock through her folds and along her clit.

"Mhmmm," she moans as I nip at her skin, soothing the sting with a lap of my tongue.

"Can I fuck you?" I ask, not wanting to just assume.

"Do you have a condom?" she asks.

Fuck, shit, god-dammit. I internally start running through things in my mind, hoping and praying that I have a condom stuck in my wallet. "Let me check," I tell her, pushing off her and sliding off the bed. I locate my jeans in the heaping pile of clothes on the floor, pulling my wallet from my back pocket. I rummage through it, looking through all of it for one. Coming up empty, I toss the offending piece of leather on the floor, pissed that I don't have one on me. "Fuck!" I curse under my breath. "Looks like we're out of luck," I grumble in my annoyance.

"Maybe check the minibar?" Carmen suggests and I spring into action. I pull every box and bottle from the area, not seeing what I need.

"Check those little boxes, maybe?" Carmen says, pointing to two small boxes on the edge of the minibar. One is a sewing kit. Who knew they still made those? Hallelujah, I could almost sing to the angels above. The second box is saving this night for me, for sure. Inside is three condoms and three packets of lube. I toss the box to Carmen, who's still on the bed, just sitting up now as she watched me clear out the minibar.

"Who would have thought the damn minibar would be saving us tonight?" I ask as I crawl back into the bed. I sit back on my haunches and stroke my cock.

"Can I?" Carmen asks, a little timidly, holding up the condom so I can see. She's already torn the package open and has the condom between her fingers.

"Fuck yes, you can," I tell her, letting go of my cock.

I watch as she reaches out for it, giving me two strokes before she places the condom over my crown and rolls it down my shaft. "God-damn your hands feel amazing," I tell her, leaning in to steal a quick kiss.

The moment our lips connect, it is like fucking fireworks go off overhead. I could seriously kiss this woman for hours, definitely every day.

With the condom firmly in place, I roll us back to how we were before, with Carmen under me. My cock slides through her folds again as I capture her lips in a bruising kiss. I roll my hips, hitting her clit with my crown, which has her moaning into my mouth. I roll them once more before I reach down, aligning myself with her entrance and then thrusting inside. I don't stop until I'm balls deep and holy-fucking-shit. I've never felt something so perfect a day in my life.

"Fuck, Carmen, you're perfect," I tell her as we break the kiss. I start out thrusting slowly, letting my cock tease her as I drag it out and quickly snap my hips to thrust back inside. I repeat this a handful of times. Each drag of my cock has Carmen digging her nails into my back. I'm sure she's drawn blood by now, but fuck it, the bite of pain is egging me on.

"Faster," she moans, and I listen. Quickening my rhythm, my hips start snapping back and forth fast as I feel her body start to flutter around my shaft. I adjust one of her legs to sit up higher on my hip, which in turn allows me to slide just a hair deeper, hitting yet another trigger spot deep inside her pussy.

"Take what you need, baby," I tell her, wanting her to use my body to reach that ultimate release. "Fuck," I growl as I feel the tingle at the base of my spine start to strengthen before it slides down into my balls and shaft.

It all happens too quickly, I'm not even sure I know what happens first, but I do know that I come so hard I see stars behind my eyes as I empty into the condom with Carmen's body milking me as she comes hard.

I roll our sweat-slick bodies as I collapse onto the bed. I didn't want to crush her and that is exactly what would have happened had I collapsed on top.

I kiss her shoulder as I attempt to suck in a few calming breaths. "You good?" I ask once my breathing has returned to almost normal.

"Yeah," she says, pushing up from the bed. I watch as she starts to walk out of the room.

"Where are you going?" I call out, just as I hear the bathroom door snick shut. I stay on the bed, sprawled out with every part of my body on display, hoping she'll return, and we can do that all again.

TWELVE

CARMEN

"*WHAT THE FUCK, WHAT THE FUCK, WHAT THE FUCK*" I chant to myself as I stand at the bathroom sink looking at my reflection in the mirror. What did I just do? Why did I just let Lucas ravish my body like he did? That man is talented. My body has never felt so good, nor do I think I've ever come that hard. I'm not usually one that can orgasm during intercourse, so the fact that I did is saying something.

I sit down and pee quickly. The last thing I need while on the road is a UTI. I contemplate jumping in the shower to wash off the sex sweat, but wonder if that would be more awkward with Lucas still in my room. I grab the fluffy hotel robe from the back of the door, wrapping it around my body before I open the bathroom door and walk back into the room.

I'm a confident, bad-ass woman. There is no reason I should feel any shame for just having sex, possibly the best ever. So, I hold my head high and walk back into the bedroom. I grab a hair tie from my bag as I walk past it, pulling my hair up into a messy bun on the top of my head.

"Everything okay?" Lucas asks, his sexy voice causing my lady bits to tingle.

"Yea-Yes," I correct myself. *Remember, you are a bad-ass and confident woman. Do not feel shame.* My inner voice encourages me as I step closer to the bed. The same one that Lucas is still sprawled out on; did I mention he's still gloriously naked? Every last drool worthy inch of him is on display to me and I, all of a sudden, have a craving to run my tongue along the ridges of his abs.

"Carmen." He says my name, pulling me from my trance. *Shit. I'm so busted checking him out.*

"Yes?" I say, more question-like than statement as I shift my eyes up to meet his. He's got a shit-eating grin filling his face, seeing as he just busted me checking him out.

"See something you like, Red? You're more than welcome to come back for round two," he says, tapping the bed beside him as he rolls onto his side. I can't help but allow my eyes to follow the length of his body as he moves. My eyes widen when I stop on his cock. He's hard again and I can feel the slickness between my thighs in response.

"Maybe," I breathily reply. I flick my eyes back to his and watch as they dilate as I flick my tongue across my bottom lip to moisten it. The sexual tension is practically crackling between us and I can tell now that it is inevitable that we'll end up in another jumbled, tangled mess of limbs, sooner if the look in Lucas's eyes is any indication.

"Why don't you come back over here, lose the robe on the way, and sit on my face. Let me make you feel really good," he says, my eyes falling once more as he starts stroking his cock.

"How?" I ask, pointing to his cock.

"How what, baby?" he asks.

"How are you able to go again and so quickly?" I ask in astonishment. I've never been with a guy that had any rebound time, much less within an hour.

"Easy, Red," he says, using that damn nickname that pisses me off just as much as it turns me on—not that I'll ever tell him that. "Stamina. I've got it in spades. Haven't you seen me out on the field?"

"Some," I admit. "But I don't ever get to watch a game from start to end. I'm always busy with something and only get to catch bits and pieces."

He holds out a hand, encouraging me to come join him. I pull the belt free, allowing the robe to fall from my shoulders. I drop it to the floor, standing still for a few seconds as it pools at my feet.

"You are so fucking gorgeous," he muses, and it causes me to blush. "Red," his voice drops an octave and gets all gravely, "get your pretty ass over here. Now. Or I'm going to spank the shit out of it."

I do as instructed, walking to the edge of the bed. I place a knee on the mattress, sliding on as seductively as possible. "Like this?" I ask.

"Yes, now get your sexy ass up here and let me eat

your pussy," he says as he slides his hands under my arms and helps guide me up the bed and to where he wants me.

"Lucas," I try and scold him, but it comes out all breathless seeing how his tongue just connected with my clit.

"Relax and just let your body enjoy," he says after sliding me off his mouth for a second. "I can feel just how tense you are, and if you don't let go of that, you won't enjoy this like you should."

"That's easier said than done," I tell him. I look down and blush a deeper shade of red at the sight of him beneath me. This is a first for me, so I will my body to relax and just enjoy this. I'm going to need to enjoy it while it's happening, because as soon as he walks out my hotel room door, it can't and won't happen again.

"That's it," he praises, "now, just let your body feel," he tells me before sucking my clit back between his lips. I do as he says and just let my body feel. I've never been very adventurous in the bedroom, never been with someone that wanted much more than missionary, maybe the occasional time with me on top or a few seconds of doggy. So being with Lucas like this is a whole new experience for me, one that, I have to admit, I'm really enjoying now that I've let my body relax and get into it. Before I even realize it, my hips are rolling as he works my body over. He's slid a few fingers inside my pussy as his tongue does some incredible things to my clit, which has me soaring over the cliff as my orgasm crashes through my body. I come so hard; my entire body is shaking as I fall forward, no longer having the strength to hold myself up.

I'm in the best post-orgasm haze. I can feel Lucas shifting around as he slides out from beneath me and goes up behind me, pressing his hard body against my back. I can feel his hard as a bat cock nestled against the crack of my ass, but am surprised when he doesn't attempt to do anything except hold me as I come down from my intense orgasm.

I swipe some hairs from my forehead that had fallen from my messy bun. "Feeling okay?" Lucas whispers, his lips mere centimeters from my ear.

"Never been better, but I might be a bit sore later. Your scruff did a number on my lady bits," I tell him honestly, now that I'm feeling the aftermath.

"Come with me," he says, rolling over and out of the bed. I look over my shoulder at him. He's standing at the edge of the bed, his hand out for me to take. I roll over, sitting at the edge of the bed for a second before I attempt to stand. Once I'm confident my legs will hold me, I stand and take his offered hand. I have no clue what he's planning, but something tells me I can trust him.

Lucas leads me into the oversized bathroom my suite happens to have and flips the plug to the jetted tub before he turns the water on to start filling it. I watch in amazement as he adds some of the bath salts that are on the ledge, then grabs two towels and places them on the floor next to the tub. He turns back to me, offering me his hand and I step up next to him at the edge of the tub. "Let's relax and soak. It will help with the soreness." I'm a little in awe at his tenderness. I stay rooted in my spot as he steps into the hot water. I know it is hot just from the steam that is rising from it. I take his offered hand again and step in. We both sit down, him behind me with his large body cradling me. Once we're seated, he reaches over and shuts the water off and hits the button to start the jets now that we've got enough water for them to run correctly.

We lay there in the bath for a while, the silence never feeling awkward or heavy. I could almost fall asleep like this. A warm body holding me like I'm the most important asset it has to protect.

"Feeling better?" he finally asks, breaking the silence. I watch as he cups water in his large hand, then lets it run down my chest and over my breasts.

"Yes, I'm ready for bed now," I tell him.

"Do you want to get out?" he asks, shifting slightly underneath me.

"No," I tell him honestly and can feel him chuckle.

"We can stay as long as you want. Or until the water goes completely cold," he says.

"Five more minutes," I tell him.

I watch as he stops with the water over my breasts, his hand coming to rest on my abdomen. His hands are so large, they cover my entire rib cage from just under my breasts to my hip bone. I don't know what it is about having them on me, but it is such a comfort, one that I've longed for, for a while now.

My five minutes pass by, plus some, before we finally move to get out of the tub. I'm now water-logged, sexed happy, and extremely tired. I let Lucas wrap the fluffy towel around my body, loving how he tenderly tucks the end between my breasts to keep the towel in place. "Let's get you into bed," he suggests, leaning down and placing a kiss on the corner of my mouth. I walk out of the bathroom, not really knowing what to expect. Do I ask him to stay? Would he even want to stay?

"I can practically hear you thinking from over here." He chuckles at me.

"Sorry, I'm just not sure what's next, or what's the protocol, or what you're thinking," I ramble on, not making much sense.

I stop at my suitcase and pull out a clean pair of panties and my sleep set.

Lucas walks up behind me and takes the items from my hands before tossing them onto the bed. He turns me in his arms and tips my head up to look at him. I see so many things swimming in his blue eyes. Lust. Want. But I also see some hesitation, maybe a little worry mixed in, as well. I've always thought that he was this over-confident and often cocky man, but maybe that is just a façade. "What comes next is up to us. There is no protocol. We're both adults. We can decide for ourselves what we want, where we stand. I'm not saying this is forever, but I can tell you that I've enjoyed getting to know you better lately and I want to get to know you even more. We've proven tonight that we connect on an intimate level," he says, and that devilish smirk returns to his lips. "One I wouldn't mind exploring more," he says, then lowers his head to place a kiss on the corner of my mouth.

"But for now, how about we get some sleep. We can see how we feel in the morning."

"Okay," I finally agree. "Does that mean that you're staying the night?"

"Unless you kick me out, I plan on laying my head on that pillow over there and holding you in my arms all night," he says, and I about melt into a puddle at his feet.

Instead, he steps away from me, closing the distance over to the bed, and holds up my clothes. I follow him, slipping my panties on before dropping the towel. I slip my shorts and tank top on, as well. "I need to brush my teeth before I get into bed," I tell him and pad off to the bathroom. I rush through my nighttime routine before returning to the bedroom. "I found a hotel toiletry kit in the bathroom with a toothbrush, if you wanted one," I tell him.

"Thanks, I'll go get myself ready," he says. I watch his tight ass—unfortunately, it is now covered by the fabric of his boxer briefs, so at least it's being showcased nicely—as he walks away. I bite my lower lip to stop myself from either moaning or drooling at the sight of it. Once Lucas is out of the room and my line of vision, I pull back the sheets and adjust the pillows on my side of the bed. I slip between the cold sheets, loving the crisp feeling of them on my skin. I'm still a little warm from the hot water we soaked in for so long, that the coldness from the sheets feels so good against my hot skin.

THIRTEEN

LUCAS

I wake up, still a little shocked I ended up in Carmen's room, naked, with her coming on my cock and tongue multiple times last night. It was so much better than I could have ever imagined it to be, especially once I got her to relax and just feel.

I can't see a clock from the way I'm lying on the bed with Carmen tucked into me. I know it's early since it is still dark outside.

I slip from the bed, needing to piss. I take care of business, find my phone, and make sure that I didn't miss anything important while I've been a little occupied with Carmen. I don't find anything pressing, so I set an alarm on my phone, then set it on the nightstand before I slide back into bed and curl around Carmen once again. I haven't slept this soundly in forever. Being with her last night was so much more than I ever could have expected. I can only hope it wasn't a one-time thing. Something tells me she isn't the one-night stand kind of woman. I start thinking of ways I can convince her to give me a shot as I drift off to sleep for another few hours.

"Lucas!" Carmen screeches my name and she suddenly sits up. I crack my eyes open and see the panic on her face as she looks at me and around the room. The sun has come up, now, bathing the room in lots of light.

"What's wrong?" I ask, trying to reach out and pull her back into my arms, but fail when she bats my hands away.

"I have an eight thirty meeting," she says, all flustered as she tries to untangle her body from the sheets.

"What time is it?" I ask as I roll over and reach for my phone. Apparently, I had my phone on silence and the seven thirty alarm I set went off but we didn't hear it. I see that it is already eight fifteen, so at least she isn't late for the meeting yet. "Shit," I mutter, rolling myself out of the bed. "What can I do to help?" I ask as she starts to run around, grabbing clothes from her suitcase before disappearing into the bathroom.

"I don't know!" she cries from the other side of the closed door. I can hear the water running and the rustling of her moving around, probably trying to do her hair and put on makeup at the same time.

"How about some coffee and breakfast. I can put in an order for the Starbucks downstairs and run down to get it if you tell me what you want," I offer.

I pull up the app, and the door to the bathroom flies open. "You're a godsend," she says, already dressed in a pencil skirt and blouse with some fuck-me heels that have my dick twitching in my boxer briefs. "I'll take a Grande

White Mocha with an extra shot of espresso, no whip cream and a breakfast sandwich, the bacon Gouda one, if they have it," she says, pulling me from my dirty thoughts. I punch all of that into the app, sending the order in while I go in search of my clothes.

"Do you want me to bring it back up here to the room, or just meet you in the lobby?" I ask as I slip my shoes on. She's down to about seven minutes until her meeting starts, so hopefully it is somewhere close by.

"Can you bring it to the meeting room next to the banquet room the team meals are in?" she asks.

"Sure can," I tell her, slipping my phone into my back pocket. I tug her to me, dropping a chaste kiss on her lips before I step back. "Try not to panic, it will slow you down. And you look gorgeous, even if you only had ten minutes to get ready," I tell her and then turn and walk away. It takes a few minutes for me to reach the Starbucks that is in the lobby of the hotel. Thankfully, my order is waiting for me when I walk up, so I'm able to grab it quickly and then head up to the second floor where I told her I'd meet her. I find the room easily and meet her at the doorway. "These are for you. Text me when you're done?" I ask, handing over the cup and sandwich.

"Yeah, sure. And Lucas, thanks," she says, and her cheeks deepen at the double meaning of her words.

"No need to thank me, Red. I'll see you later." I wink at her and walk away. I need a shower and some breakfast of my own, and I should probably plug my phone in, so I don't miss her text message later today.

"Where did you disappear to last night?" Matt O'Riley asks after I sit down in one of the lounges the hotel has provided for the team. They've got all kinds of entertainment options going on in here for us, seeing how we have so much downtime between games right now.

"I don't kiss and tell, man." I smirk at him and run my fingers through my still damp hair from the quick shower I grabbed before coming to find my teammates.

"Since when?" he retorts.

"Since I said so," I tell him, my tone advising him to drop it. What I did last night with Carmen isn't up for discussion, especially with my teammates. My night with her is only for us, and I find myself wanting to protect that privacy at all cost.

"Damn, man, calm down." He smirks. "How's Carmen this morning?" he asks, and it's obvious he's put two and two together, since he knows I escorted her back to her room last night.

"Last I knew, she was in a meeting this morning," I tell him, and hope he'll drop the questioning.

I luck out when Derek and JJ come into the room, both sitting down with us. "What's up, guys?" Matt asks them both.

"Nothing much, just waiting on my wife to call once the kids are napping," Derek says. You can almost feel how much he hates being away from his wife and kids when we're on the road. "What's up with you guys?" he asks.

"What you see," I tell him. "Anyone want to hit up the gym?" I ask, needing something to do that will get some energy out. My knees won't stop bouncing while I'm sitting here, and I think it's because I have so much built-up energy and excitement. It's coursing through my blood.

We sit around, shooting the shit, until Derek gets the call he'd been waiting on from his wife. Once he finishes up talking to her, we pick up our trash and head out of the lounge.

"Damn, this place is nice!" JJ says as we push through the doors of the hotel's gym. It looks newly renovated with machines that look brand new.

"Yeah, it is," I agree with him. I head for a treadmill, first, to get in a warmup run before I hit the weights.

"Damn, boy. How much weight are you trying to press?" Derek asks as he steps in to spot me.

"Just my normal three fifty," I tell him before I remove the bar from the rack and start my first rep.

I finish up in the weight room with the guys and am ready to head for my hotel room for my second shower of the day.

"Hey, Lucas," Matt calls out to catch my attention.

I stop in the doorway, turning around to look at him, and find him across the room from me. "What?" I call out.

"You want to grab some lunch with us?" he asks.

"Maybe, I'll text you once I'm done showering. I need to make a call afterwards, first," I tell him, since I want to try and check in with Carmen and see if she's done with her meeting so we can have lunch together. I'd rather do that with her than the guys.

He just smirks at me from across the hall, probably knowing damn well why I won't commit to lunch with the guys. "All right, text me later, then."

I head to my room, stripping from my sweaty clothes as soon as I enter the room and the door shuts behind me. I step under the hot spray and let the water work its magic on my sore muscles. Once I'm relaxed, I wash up, then step out of the shower. Once I'm all dried off, I wrap the towel around my waist and stand at the bathroom sink. I pull out my razor and clean up my beard. I like to keep it on the shorter side so that it doesn't get out of hand.

Once finished in the bathroom, I pull a pair of joggers, a T-shirt, and a pair of boxer briefs from my bag and take them over to my bed to get dressed. I sit on the bed, sans shirt, and grab my cell from the nightstand. I pull up my text messages, and hover over Carmen's name for a few seconds, trying to decide if I should send her a message or just wait for her to come to me. I'm not here to pressure her into anything, even if we were perfect for each other last night.

Fuck it, I think as I hit her contact and type in a quick message.

Lucas: Will you be free for lunch?

I toss my phone on the bed next to me while I pull my shirt on then kick back and turn the TV on. I'm sure Carmen is busy in her meeting, so I don't really expect to hear from her until it is almost time.

I flip on ESPN, watching some sports highlights while I pass the time. My phone buzzes next to me, so I flip my phone over and see my sister and nephew's faces on the screen. I hit accept and they both fill my phone's screen.

"Uncle Lucas!" Milo practically screams when he sees me.

"What's up, buddy?"

"I's had to have pokes today," he says as he sticks his bottom lip out in an exaggerated pout.

"I'm sorry to hear that, buddy," I tell him. I hate that he has gone through so much in his short life already. He was born prematurely and has had health complications since. Thankfully, once he made it out of the NICU after a two-month stay, he's not had any life-threatening issues, but more so just lingering complications due to being premature. He has a feeding tube that they are working to get him off of, but have to go through food therapy, first, which wasn't easy. Everything would make him puke, due to the textures. Because of his complications, he has to get regular bloodwork and other tests done to make sure that he's staying as healthy as possible. The doctors are all predicting that he'll eventually outgrow most of these things, it just takes time. "How many pokes did you get?" I ask him.

"Two," he says, his lip quivering.

"Aww, I bet you were a superhero, though."

"I got a sucker and then Mommy took me for ice cream!" he says, the quivering lip gone, and a smile plastered on his face once again. He learned quickly that he loved ice cream, so it often becomes a reward when he has to have doctors or therapy appointments.

"A sucker and ice cream? Man, you must have been a good boy!" I praise him. There have been many days that I'd get calls from Tiffany as she sobbed after a hard day of him screaming through a therapy appointment or having to be pinned down just for them to take blood. Once I got called up to Indianapolis, it has allowed me to come and help her sometimes. The day he broke his leg and had to have surgery was the day of the fan event that I blew off because my family comes first. Maybe I should explain to Carmen why I missed that event, not that it would change anything since it was weeks ago, but at least she'd know why I wasn't there.

"You ready for game one tonight?" Tiffany asks as Milo slides off her lap and disappears out of view.

"I think so, had a good morning and now I'm just hanging out in my hotel room relaxing. Will head out for some lunch here, soon," I tell her, just as a text notification pops up at the top of my screen. I can't read all of it but can tell that it is Carmen texting me back, so I grab my iPad from the bedside table and pull up my messages.

"What's that smile for?" Tiffany asks, always the observant one.

"I just got a reply from someone I was waiting to hear back from," I tell her.

"Oh god, please don't tell me you have a booty call that lives in each city." She grimaces.

"Damn, jumping to savage right off the bat." I chuckle and bring my eyes back to the camera so I can give her my '*not amused*' look. "But no, not a booty call. It was from Carmen, the team's PR person," I tell her.

"Ooh, is she the one that you have the crush on?" she pries.

"A crush, really?" I deadpan.

"No sense lying about it. I can tell you like her just by the way you, one, always bring her up when we talk. I don't even think you realize that you do it, but I have. Two, the way you say her name and the way your voice changes. It's okay, baby bro, you're allowed to like a woman. I'd actually encourage you finding someone to date, and, I don't know, maybe marry one day."

"Fuck, Tiff. That's a little fast, don't you think? I've only slept with her once," I blurt, and slam my lips together after letting that slip out.

"What!" she yells, slapping her leg or the couch or something that causes a loud smack sound. "Tell me everything, well, not *everything*, but I want all the details outside of the actual smexy times, because eww. You're my brother, I don't need to know those specifics."

Before I answer her, I look back at the text from Carmen so that I can reply.

Carmen: Sorry for the delay, I just got done
with my morning meetings. I'm free until
about two.
Lucas: Meet me for lunch?

I shoot off the question, and the bubbles immediately

pop up. "Just a second, Tiff," I tell my sister while I wait for Carmen's reply.

Carmen: Sure, can you give me twenty minutes?

Lucas: Yep, do you need longer? I'm free until the bus takes us to the stadium.

Carmen: Thanks.

Lucas: I'm in my room, just come here when you're ready, sound good?

Carmen: Sure.

Knowing that Carmen is coming to me when she's ready, I put my iPad back down and turn back to my sister. The Cheshire smile filling her pretty face tells me she is not going to let this little tidbit of information go.

"You were about to tell me all about Carmen and the fact that you've, apparently, already slept together. Why haven't you told me more about her already?" she asks, and I can tell she thinks that I've kept things from her.

"It just kind of happened," I tell her, reaching for my water and taking a quick drink before I continue. "When I first got to Indianapolis, I wasn't her favorite person. I kept doing shit that she'd have to spin. After the baby debacle, I've laid low, as you well know, and did my best to stay out of her radar. When we have been around each other, I've tried to make it a pleasurable time. I sat next to her on the flight here and we talked for a good chunk of it. Then, the guys convinced her to come hang out with us last night. I'm confident the attraction goes both ways. So, anyway, the tension kept building last night and, well, I offered to walk her to her room at the end of the night, and let's just say, we didn't part ways until this morning. Now, we're meeting up for lunch once she gets here to my room," I tell my sister, filling her in on everything that has transpired.

"Damn," she says, waving her hand in front of her face like she's hot.

I quirk an eyebrow at her. "Damn, what?" I ask, hoping she'll elaborate.

"I've just never seen you get all dreamy over a woman, and you went dreamy when you just told me all of that. This one has got you all wrapped up and it's only been a few hours. The fact that you are having lunch today is very telling."

I hear a soft knock on the door, my eyes going in that direction like I can see through the wall. "Gotta go," I say. "I'll call you tomorrow. Give Milo my love," I tell her as I jump off the bed and head for the door.

"Don't do anything stupid! I want this one to last long enough so that I can meet her," she says before I disconnect the call in time to open the door.

I about swallow my tongue when my eyes land on Carmen. She's obviously gone back to her room, as she looks freshly showered. She has on minimal makeup with her hair pulled up into a ponytail, is wearing some tight ass jeans, a team polo and chucks. If she isn't the fantasy of every red-blooded male on this planet, I don't know what they're thinking, because standing in front of me is the most beautiful woman I've laid my eyes on.

"Hi," she greets, and it comes out a little shy or breathlessly. I can't tell which one just yet.

"Hi, want to come in?" I ask, stepping back and opening the door all the way. I swing my arm in a welcoming gesture.

She bites her bottom lip as she looks both ways down the hall. I have to bite back a groan at what that lip bite does to my cock. I've also never been more jealous of someone biting their own damn lip.

"Sure," she finally says and steps over the threshold of my room. I normally wouldn't ever have a woman up in my room while on a road trip. Management frowns on that, but since Carmen has access to this floor, I know I wouldn't get in trouble for having sneaked a woman up here.

"How were your meetings?" I ask as I move about my room. I slip on some socks and shoes before I grab my phone, wallet and then slide a baseball hat onto my head.

"Good!" she says, lighting up. "We went over everything for this afternoon and evening."

"Anyone realize that you were coming in at the last minute?" I ask, knowing that she was panicking after waking up late this morning.

"Nope, we actually started about twenty minutes late because a few other people were running late, so no one noticed that I wasn't ready on time," she tells me.

"Shall we?" I ask, now that I'm ready to head out.

"Yep, where did you want to go? I'm guessing not the team's lounge?" she questions as we step out into the hall.

"If you're okay with leaving, it looks like there's an Italian place a block or two away that we can walk to."

"That sounds perfect," she tells me as we get onto the elevator. I send a quick text to Matt, letting him know I won't be joining the guys for lunch today.

We walk the few blocks to the restaurant, our conversation flowing easily on our way.

As soon as we're seated, a waiter approaches and goes over the specials. We end up ordering one of their wood fired pizzas to split.

"So," Carmen starts to say once the server walks away. She picks up the water glass the young girl set down and takes a sip before returning it to the cardboard coaster it was set on. "About last night." She worries her lip as she takes her time.

"Was special and a night I'll never forget," I interject. I can see the writing on the wall, here, she's ready to claim it was a mistake and can't ever happen again. I beg to differ.

"Wait, what?" she asks, the surprise evident in her question.

"Last night was one of the best nights I've ever had, and I'm not just saying that to blow smoke up your ass. You can't deny that there is a mutual attraction between the two of us. I've felt it and I'm confident in my assessment that you've felt it. Last night was explosive. It was special and something I hope we can pursue," I tell her, laying it all on the line.

I watch as Carmen opens and closes her mouth a couple times, obviously trying to figure out how she's going to reply. I give her the time she needs, as she's obviously struggling with what to say.

She reaches for her glass once again, this time draining half of the glass of water before replacing it on the coaster.

"Talk to me, Red," I plead, tossing in my nickname for her that I know riles her up.

Her eyes pop up from the table to meet my own. I can see that spark of hers come to life as she straightens her spine and readies herself.

"We can't do this, Lucas," she starts, pointing between the two of us. "I won't deny that I'm attracted to you, and last night was not expected, it can't happen again."

"Why can't it happen again?" I press, wanting to know why she feels that way.

"A few reasons, one, I don't date players. Especially players it is my job to represent on behalf of the team. Second, we are co-workers, in a sense. Yes, we work in completely different departments, but I still work with everyone on the team on a regular basis. What happens when word gets out and things get weird, who is the team going to replace, the PR person or one of their star players? I cannot lose this job. I've worked my ass off to get to where I am. Not to mention that I'm not looking for a good time fling. I'm ready to look towards my future. I want to settle down and start a family. I know I'm only two years older than you, but I feel like that two years makes a difference in where we are at in our lives."

She pauses again and I look over my shoulder at what has pulled her attention. Our sever arrives at that moment, setting our piping hot pizza down between the two of us, along with two plates. "Can I get you guys anything else?" she asks.

"Can I get a lemonade and a side of ranch, please?" Carmen asks.

"Of course, and you, sir?" She turns my way.

"I'm good, thanks," I tell her as I reach for a slice and place it on my plate. I top it with some parmesan before I take a large bite. The server was spot on when she suggested we get their famous pizza.

"Holy crap that is good," Carmen says after her first bite.

"Yeah, it is." I take another large bite, cramming in half of my slice in the one bite.

We both focus on eating our pizza, our conversation set aside due to how good it is. Once we've both devoured a few slices each, I bring us back to the conversation at hand.

"I understand your concern about the work aspect, but I don't really see it as a deal breaker. It isn't against the rules, from what I remember," I tell her, pausing to take another bite. "And if we decided to see where things could go and we realize that it isn't what we're hoping for, I don't see why we can't both be adults about it and part as friends. No one needs to lose a job over a breakup."

"I don't know, Lucas," Carmen interjects, worry filling her expression.

"What if I suggested keeping it casual, just between the two of us. Nothing public for a while. It would give us time to get to know one another on a deeper level."

She looks across the table at me and I can tell her mind is spinning at a hundred miles an hour as she thinks over my suggestion.

"So, you want me to be your booty call?" she deadpans, rolling her eyes at me. "Yeah, that isn't happening. I'm not into the friends with benefits scene."

"Not friends with benefits. We'd be exclusive, but just keep it between us or whoever you're comfortable knowing that we're dating. I'll be up front that there is no way I'll be able to hide it from my sister. She already figured out that something happened between the two of us just by talking to me today." I smirk, thinking back to my conversation with Tiffany.

"Not to be rude, but have you ever had an exclusive relationship?" she asks.

I can't help but laugh at her question; I mean, I get it. I'm not known for relationships and have been in the news more for my strip club shenanigans, then the baby daddy accusations. I don't paint the best image for her to latch on to. "I had a serious girlfriend for two years in college until I walked in on her and one of the football players. I swore off relationships for a long time after that, not wanting the distraction or possibility of getting my heart broken again. I really thought she was the one, but I was sorely mistaken. Apparently, she was sleeping around with lots of jocks, and I was just in the dark about it."

"I'm sorry," Carmen says, reaching across the table and placing her hand on top of mine. I appreciate the gesture and warmth of her hand on mine. "No one ever deserves to be cheated on, I know what it's like to have that happen and it makes you wonder if you'll ever trust another person again."

Knowing that she's been cheated on, as well, has my blood pressure rising and wondering if I can find the man that hurt her so I can punch him in the face, or maybe I need to buy him a drink for fucking things up so I have the chance at winning her over.

"Going back to your original argument, I'm definitely not opposed to settling down, I just want it to be with the right woman. Seeing my sister become a mom and then being around my nephew whenever I can be, made me realize that I do want kids of my own. So, don't count me out on those matters. I also think it's sexy as hell that I could be dating an older woman." I wink at her, and love watching her skin pinken at my words.

"I still don't know, Lucas." She bites that god-damned lip again and my cock twitches to life in my pants.

"What if we gave ourselves two months to see how things go. If at the end of that time, it isn't what you want going forward, then we part as friends and I won't say another word about it."

"How can you be so confident that if we part ways that we can do so without broken hearts and hurt feelings?"

"Because I don't plan on that happening. I want to see where this connection between us can go. I want to see it blossom and grow. Carmen, you are an incredible woman. You are confident. You are sexy. You are what I see in my future and I want to be the man who stands beside you to be your confidant and support system when you need it, and your biggest cheerleader."

"Wow," she says a little breathlessly. "You sure know how to win a woman over with words." She smiles at me.

"So, does that mean you'll agree to dating me?" I ask, slipping my hand from under hers and linking our fingers together. I don't think she even realized she still had her hand on mine.

"I guess so," she says, and I want nothing more than to pull her into my arms and kiss the fuck out of her. But we're in public and have a table between the two of us, so it'll will have to wait.

"Ready to get out of here?" I ask, looking down at the time on my phone. The bus to the stadium doesn't leave for another two and a half hours, which gives us plenty of time to make it back to the hotel and for some time alone in one of our rooms.

FOURTEEN

CARMEN

I can't wipe the smile from my face, nor can I believe that I just agreed to date Lucas. The way he poured out his heart trying to convince me had me melting into a puddle. He's surprised me the last few weeks, and especially the last twenty-four hours. When I woke up this morning, I was panicking that I'd fucked up. Sleeping with him on a whim is not my normal. I don't just go sleeping around. I don't necessarily have a specific rule to when I'll sleep with a guy, but I can say that last night was a first for me.

Lucas waves down the server and gets our check, handing over some cash before she can even leave the table. "Keep the change, and thanks for the suggestion. The pizza was as good as you said it would be," he tells her before we both get up. His hand settles on my lower back as we walk through the crowded restaurant and outside onto the sidewalk. I need for us to keep this on the downlow, so as much as I want to slip my hand into his and feel his warm skin on mine, I slip them into my pockets as we walk back to the hotel.

"Do you have to do anything before leaving for the stadium?" he asks as we walk back.

"Nope," I tell him, popping the p. "I'm free until then."

"Good." He smirks and lowers his face until his lips are next to my ear as we wait at an intersection for the crosswalk to change. "I've got plans for you, then, your room or mine?" he asks, nipping at my ear.

His voice is deep and gritty as he asks, and it has my core clenching at the thought of what he has planned.

"Mine," I tell him. "It isn't near any of the players' rooms, so we'll be less likely to be seen together," I tell him, but also think to myself about people possibly hearing us if things get as loud as they did last night.

"You've got it," he says before standing back to his full height. His hand is still against my lower back as we cross the street and enter into the hotel. I don't really pay attention to who might be in the lobby or bar, we head straight for the elevator. I swipe my card and press the button for our secured floor.

As soon as the elevator doors close, our control snaps. Lucas backs me up against the wall, his lips crashing against mine as I wrap my arms around his neck and pull him down. He presses his hard body against mine, pinning me in a way that I can feel every glorious inch of his that touches me.

The ping of the elevator arriving on our floor pulls

me from the trance his kiss put me into, and I pull back. "Damn you taste good," he says, before dropping a chaste kiss on my lips before fully stepping back just as the doors slide open. It's a good thing he stepped back, as when they open, a couple of the training staff and position coaches are all standing on the other side, waiting on the doors to open so they can get on.

"Carmen, Lucas." One of them, I'm not really sure who, exactly, greets us.

"Gentlemen," I squeak as I exit the elevator. I can only imagine how red my cheeks are at almost being caught by all of them.

"Slow down, Red," Lucas says, "they didn't see anything." He smirks as he stops behind me while I open my door.

"We have to be more careful. No more kissing in elevators," I reprimand him.

"How about in locked hotel rooms?" He smirks, lifting me up like I'm nothing as he pins me to the wall as the door snicks shut.

"Hotel rooms are a yes," I tell him as his lips connect with my neck. I can't help the moan that falls from my lips at the way he plays my body, and we're still fully dressed and have hardly even made it past first base.

"Something you like?" He pulls his head back and smirks at me.

"Don't be an ass." I laugh at him and pull his face back to mine. "And don't tease me too long, I'm going to combust," I tell him just before we kiss again.

I don't know if it is the sexual drought that I'd been in

or if it is Lucas, but I swear my inner sex goddess comes out. I can't get him naked or inside of me fast enough. My body craves his like it is my next drink and I've been parched for a long time.

"Slow down, Red." He nips at my lips. "I've got to grab a condom," he tells me as he sets me back on my feet. He grabs one, rolling it down his shaft in one quick motion before picking me back up and pinning me to the wall. His cock slides against my clit and I shudder in anticipation and want.

"Lucas, I need you," I moan. He lines himself up and thrusts home. My back arches off the wall, and he's so deep I swear he's touching my ovaries.

"Tell me what you need, Red," he says before latching on to my neck with his lips. His hips start a fast rhythm as he slides in and out of my pussy. I'm quickly building to my orgasm, needing it as much as I need my next breath.

"Faster, right there," I manage to tell him. I slip my hand between our sweat-slicked bodies and circle my clit with my fingers, applying the perfect pressure that sends me flying over the edge.

"Fuck, Carmen!" he groans, thrusting through my orgasm as he crests over his own, filling the condom with his release. His forehead rests against mine, as we both suck in deep breaths as we come down from the high of endorphins coursing through our bodies.

"That was—" he says, pausing to suck in another breath.

"The best wall sex I've ever had," I finish for him.

Chuckling, he lifts me off of him, then sets me on the floor before he disposes of the condom. I can't get enough of seeing his body naked. All the glorious ridges his muscles create from the hours he's spent in a gym. He's not the over-done body builder type, but the 'I like taking care of my body and have muscles' kind of body.

"See something you like?" he asks, coming back from the bathroom. He hands over a warm washcloth and it surprises me slightly. I've never had a guy want to take care of me like this after having sex.

"Um, yeah. Have you seen yourself naked?" I ask, giving him another once over.

He looks down his body, running his hand down his abs before looking back as me. "A time or two." He smirks and brings a hand to my lower back, pulling me flush against him. "But I'd rather look at yours instead. I'm a little infatuated by it. I think I need more time to get to know it on a more intimate level," he says before picking me up and taking me to the bed.

"Once was enough before your game tonight." I smack his chest.

"I wasn't going to try for round two right now. I was just bringing you over here to cuddle until we have to get ready to go," he says, settling in against the pillows.

"Oh, well then, let me put on some clothes," I tell him.

"Clothes defeat the purpose of naked cuddling," he says, holding me tighter to him.

"I thought the purpose of naked cuddling was to end up having sex?" I question.

"That's one of the purposes, but it can also be like this," he says, and I relax into his embrace. "It also allows me to have free range to tease the fuck out of you in the meantime." He chuckles as his hands start to roam my body. "Do you remember how I missed that fan event you put together a while back, but Coach talked you off the cliff because of it?" he suddenly asks.

"Yeah?" I'm not really sure where he's going with this or why he'd bring it up now.

"The reason I missed the event was because my nephew was in the hospital and I was there with him and my sister. He was having a bad day of tests and she needed some backup. He'll usually calm down if I show up. That's why I missed. Not because I was trying to be an ass and not show up."

"Oh, Lucas," I gasp. "I didn't know that your nephew was sick, is he going to be okay?" I ask.

"Yeah, he was premature and has some lingering complications. Nothing life threatening, but he still has to see doctors on a regular basis and have tests done."

"Wow, I can't imagine what all that entails."

"It's been a rough three years for Tiffany and Brad, but they've handled it as best as any parents can. I think it strengthened their relationship. Having each other to lean on during the most stressful times. Watching them make it through Milo's birth and subsequent hospital stay, and how they leaned on one another, showed me how important it is for your spouse to be one of your best friends. You need to be able to lean on one another during the hard times."

"Thank you for sharing with me. Maybe I'll forgive you, now, for missing the event," I muse.

"Forgive me?" He laughs, tickling my side and rolling me until he's hovering over me.

"Yep," I say before his lips take mine in a kiss.

We spend the next hour making out like teenagers, but he never tries to take it any further. We finally have to pull apart when the alarm on my phone starts going off. After my close call this morning, I set alarms for everything I have to be at for the rest of the trip. No way am I letting any distractions make me miss something work related.

"Where are you going?" Lucas whines as I get up to turn my alarm off.

"To turn that off and get ready. That also means that it is time for *you*," I say, pointing at him, "to go back to your room so you can get ready."

"Do I get to come back to this bed tonight?" he asks.

"Maybe." I flash him a coy smile.

"Maybe?" he scoffs.

"Score me a run and you can come back," I tell him and now I'm the one smirking at him.

"Red, I'll score you a fucking walk-off home run if that's what you want."

"Don't promise things you can't keep."

"Fair enough," he says, reaching out and grabbing my wrist and tugging on it. "Do I at least get a pre-game good luck kiss?"

"As long as one here counts," I tell him before crashing my lips to his.

"That will have to do," he muses before pulling away.

I admit I watch his every move as he gets up, pulling on his clothes. He smirks at me when he catches me checking him out yet again. "Watch it, babe, you'll make me hard again. The last thing you want me doing is getting a hard on in my baseball pants. They are already tight as it is, this," he says, pointing to the bulge in his pants, "would make them not suitable for kids to see me. It might also make some women jealous."

"You're so full of yourself," I tell him. "Most women have dildos bigger," I smart at him.

"Oh, is that right? And does that go for you, as well? Are you one of those women?" he asks, a smirk on his face, as he knows he's got me.

"Maybe," I tell him as sweetly as I can, my face burning with my embarrassment.

"Why are you turning beet red?" he asks, pulling me into his arms. "Being confident in your sexuality isn't something to be embarrassed about. I think it's fucking hot. Maybe you'll let me tease you with a toy at some point," he says.

I look up at him, a little shocked at his words. "Really? That isn't something that intimidates you?"

"Fuck no. There is nothing sexier than a woman who knows what she likes in bed and who can take matters into her own hands. If I know you as well as I think I do, I'm going to go out on a limb, here, and say that you haven't been with a man in at least a few months until last night, am I right?"

"Yeah, more like over a year," I tell him honestly.

"And I'd never expect that you wouldn't need an orgasm in that amount of time. Hell, even if we are having regular sex, you might still need one when I'm not around, and you should feel comfortable with that. There's nothing wrong with a little self-love."

"I never know what is going to come out of your mouth, but that definitely wasn't what I was expecting," I tell him.

"Make me one promise?" he asks.

"What's that?"

"I want you to promise me that you'll tell me what you want when we're intimate. If you want to try something, you tell me, you want to go somewhere—a strip club or a sex club—and we do it together. There is nothing—well, except maybe bringing other people into the bedroom with us—that I'd say no to."

"Okay," I agree. I know being open and honest with each other is important in order to build a solid relationship and that trust is important in all areas of said relationship. "Hey, thank you for trusting me enough to tell me about your nephew, earlier."

He shrugs. "I thought you should know, and I wanted to make sure you didn't have any pent-up anger over the missed event that was going to come back to bite me. But on that note, I really need to go now. I'll see you on the bus," he says, dropping a chaste kiss on my lips.

"Bye." I give him a little wave as he exits my room.

I'm floating up on cloud nine after the whirlwind the last day has been. I fall back onto the bed, just letting the memories from yesterday and today roll like credits through my mind. I can remember the anticipation of wanting him to kiss me so badly last night but not sure if he ever would. Oh, how my once hatred of the man has turned into complete lust for him.

THE NEXT FEW HOURS FLY BY IN A BLUR. WE TAKE the short ride from the hotel to the stadium, and the guys are all whisked away to the locker room and into pre-game rituals. With tonight's game being game one of the first round of the playoffs, there is a lot of ceremonial pomp and circumstance that goes on before the game even starts. Most involves the home team only, but some of it involves ours, as well, when necessary.

I help where needed, making sure everything goes off without a hitch. With the game getting prime time TV coverage, it's important things start on time.

I'm finally able to take my seat at the start of the third inning. The game is still tied at zero, but we've had some good base hits so far tonight, we just can't seem to get anyone home. Derek Smyth, one of our starting pitchers, is on the mound, and currently has thrown a perfect game. It doesn't happen often, but so far, he's on his way.

As the game goes on, my phone buzzes and I pull it out, seeing my brother is calling.

"Hey, Zach," I greet, a smile instantly filling my face.

"Hey, sis, how's it going?" he asks.

"Oh, ya know, just hard at work at a playoff game."

"Shit, that's right, the game is on right now, isn't it?" he asks.

"Yeah," I chuckle. I know he isn't a huge baseball fan, add in the time difference, his demanding job, and the fact that he has a baby at home, and he can sometimes be scatterbrained. "How are things?" I ask.

"Good, do I need to let you go? We can talk later," he offers.

"No, you're good. I'm done with my duties, for now. I'm just sitting down watching the game."

"If you're sure," Zach reiterates.

"Just spit it out, I know if you called, and not Heather, that there is a reason, brother of mine."

He laughs at me, but the sad thing is, he knows I'm right. "Okay, you've got me. I was calling to let you know that I've got two weeks of leave coming up and we wanted to come visit you for at least a week of it."

"Oh, that's awesome, do you have the dates?" I ask, mentally going through my calendar. Depending on how deep into the playoffs we go, we could be playing baseball until late October or early November if they make the World Series.

"I'm still waiting on the exact dates, but it might be closer to Thanksgiving."

"If that's the case, then that is perfect, but no matter what the dates are, I'll make it work."

"Great, I can't wait to see you," Zach says, and I know

he misses being around family. Especially now that he's got a son of his own.

"I'm so excited to get some auntie time in with my little stud muffin," I tell him, referring to my nephew Simon. "How is my little nephew?" I ask, changing the topic of conversation.

"Good, he finally started crawling today!" Zach tells me.

"Watch out! Now he'll be getting into everything!"

"Yeah, no shit. I can't just put him down on his play mat with some toys and expect him to stay put. He's on the move and, boy, is he curious," he tells me.

"I'm sure he is," I muse. The sound of the crowd groaning pulls my attention back to the game going on and I see that we just scored two runs, finally getting us on the board. "Sweet!" I call out.

"What's sweet?" Zach asks.

"Oh, sorry. We just scored two runs and have a runner on second to take the lead," I tell him.

"Cool, hope y'all win tonight," he says.

"Me too," I tell him, a smile tugging at my lips.

"I'll let you know the exact dates once I have them, but know it's on the horizon."

"Sounds good, Zach, give my love to Heather and Simon. Love all of you," I tell my brother.

"Love you, too, sis. Talk soon," he says before we end the call.

I'm all giddy, knowing that I'll be seeing my brother and his family soon-ish. It's been months since I was able to, and I know that my nephew is going to be huge compared to how little he was the last time I got to hold him.

I turn my attention back to the game, watching as the guys pull off the impressive win for game one of the series.

FIFTEEN

LUCAS

THE LAST FEW WEEKS HAVE FLOWN BY IN A BLUR. From games, to nights in with Carmen, it has all been a whirlwind. We were eliminated from the playoffs in the conference championship. It sucked, but it was an experience I'll never forget.

All the time that Carmen and I get to spend together just makes me crave her more. I love just laying in bed talking. Sharing about our pasts, talking about our future and things we want to do, or places we want to visit.

I've finally convinced her to meet my sister, so we're headed over to her place this afternoon and evening. I just know that Tiffany will love her and I'm sure will have fun trying to bust my balls and embarrass me with stories from our childhood.

"Hey, babe," I call out from Carmen's living room. While we both have our own places, one of us usually ends up at the other's place probably five nights of every week.

"Yeah?" she calls back.

"Will you be ready soon? Tiffany has texted me twice already, asking if we're on our way," I tell her.

"Oh, shit. Yeah, I'll be right out," she says.

I walk down the hall and into her bedroom and then the bathroom attached. I lean against the doorframe as I watch her messing with her makeup.

"Babe, you look gorgeous and she's going to love you, so quit worrying that everything isn't perfect."

"I just want to make a good impression," she says, looking at me through the mirror.

"And you will," I say, stepping up behind her and wrapping my arms around her torso. I bury my face in her neck, placing a kiss on the sensitive skin just beneath her ear. She shivers in my arms and I can feel the goose-bumps appear on her skin.

"Fine, I'm ready," she breathlessly says. I press against her, showing her what the little sighs and moans do to me.

"Fuck. Now I'm going to have blue balls all day," I jokingly tell her.

"I promise to take care of them when we get back, how's that sound?" she asks, turning in my arms and sliding her hands up my chest and around my neck until she can clasp her hands together behind my neck. She pulls me down and into a kiss. One that I deepen. I don't ever get enough of her. As soon as I have her, I just want her all over again. She's my drug of choice and I'll happily take hit after hit from her.

"Now, I'm really going to be hard this entire time.

When you look over and always see a bulge in my jeans, you'll know it's your fault," I say, smacking her ass before I pull her out of the bathroom.

"Are you sure this is her favorite?" Carmen asks, reading over the label on the wine bottle we stopped and picked up on our way.

"Yep, I've had to stop and get that exact kind many a times for her," I assure Carmen. She insisted she couldn't show up to meet my sister for the first time empty handed, so we settled on wine.

"Will you be this nervous when my brother comes to town next week and you get to meet him?" she asks from the passenger seat as I pull into my sister's neighborhood.

"Nope," I tell her confidently. "But I'm a guy, we don't stress over meetings like this like girls do."

"Must be nice. I've been a ball of nerves for a week," she says.

"I know, babe. Apparently, my attempts at relieving that stress haven't worked like I'd wanted them to," I tell her, referring to all the sex we've had.

"You're incorrigible." She laughs, smacking my arm. My teasing worked, since it got her smiling and laughing.

I pull into Tiffany's driveway and the front door flies open. She steps out, Milo at her side. They stay on the porch while we grab our things and exit my car.

"About time you got here," Tiffany calls out from the

porch. "You are allowed to let her out of the bedroom every once and awhile," she teases.

"Sorry we're late, it was totally my fault," Carmen says once she's out of the car.

We make it up the stairs and I scoop Milo into my arms. "Hey, buddy, miss me?" I ask my nephew before I blow a raspberry on his neck. I just saw him a couple days ago, but I still miss him when we're not around.

"Uncle Lucas." He giggles. "Stop," he insists, pushing against my face.

"Tiff." I lean in, kissing my sister on the cheek. "I'd like to finally introduce to you, Carmen. Carmen, this is my pain in the butt sister, Tiffany."

"I don't know how you put up with him, but bless you," Tiffany says as she pulls Carmen in for a hug. The way Carmen's eyes bug out in shock has me biting back a bark of laughter.

"It is so nice to meet you, as well. Thank you for having me."

"Of course, you are welcome here anytime. With or without this one," Tiffany tells her, pointing at me. "If you need someone to complain to when he's being an a-s-s," she says, spelling out the word so that Milo doesn't repeat it like he's done in the past with cuss words, "I'm your girl. I can relate. Plus, who doesn't need another girlfriend to meet up with over wine and appetizers."

"That does sound like a good time," Carmen muses.

"Can we take this party inside?" I ask, smirking at my sister.

"Oh, yes, sorry! I was just so excited for you to get

here," Tiffany says as she opens the door and steps inside. I drop a hand to the small of Carmen's back, escorting her inside with Milo on my hip.

Tiffany leads us inside and to the living room that is filled with Milo's toys. I immediately set him down and drop to the floor with him.

"Speaking of wine, this is for you." Carmen hands the bottle over to my sister.

"Thank you, this is my favorite!"

"See, I told you!" I chime in, winking at Carmen as Tiffany takes the bottle into the kitchen. "This is my special friend, Carmen, can you say hi to Miss Carmen?" I ask Milo.

He shakes his head, trying to hide into my arm. He's often shy around new people, but I'm sure before we leave today, he'll be just as smitten with her as I am.

"Milo, do you have a favorite toy?" Carmen asks him, getting down on the floor with us.

He looks between me and Carmen, not really sure what to make of her. He eventually leaves my side and goes and gets a couple of his cars. We've played endless hours of cars. For Christmas last year, I found this awesome rug that has all kinds of roads on it to roll cars around on. He hands one to me and, shocking both of us, hands one to Carmen, as well.

"Thank you, Milo. This is such an awesome car!" she exclaims, a little over exaggerated, which gets him smiling. He sits down between us and starts rolling his own car along one of the roadways on the rug. Carmen follows suit, zooming her car down one of the other roads.

When Tiffany joins us again, she finds the three of us zooming cars all over the mat. "Well, looks like he's already won you over," she muses, taking a seat on the recliner.

"You feeling okay, Tiff?" I ask, noticing that she's looking a little pale.

"Yeah, just a stomach bug, I think. It's been hitting me randomly the last couple of days."

I'm no expert, but random bouts of nausea screams pregnant, to me, but I don't want to be the asshole that asks her, so I keep my mouth shut. "Sorry, do you want to go take a nap while we play with Milo?" I offer.

"Really? You don't mind?" she asks, sitting up straight like the idea of a nap is the greatest thing she's ever heard of.

"Go, take a nap, or a shower, or both. You deserve it!" Carmen tells her. "I don't know how you do it all the time. Being a stay-at-home mom sounds exhausting."

"It can be, but it's also amazing to be here for all his big moments," Tiff says as she stands to go.

"If I'm not up in two hours, come wake me up. I don't want to sleep too long and then not be able to sleep tonight."

"You got it," I assure my sister.

"Milo, you be good for Uncle Lucas and Miss Carmen while Mommy goes and takes a nap."

"Okay," he answers her, not really giving a crap that she's leaving the room.

"He had a small feed about twenty minutes before you got here, so he should be good for a while. We've got some finger foods to try at lunch, before we do another feed, depending on how much he can get down."

"Sounds good, I'll come get you before attempting to feed him if he says he's hungry."

"Perfect. Thanks again," she says before disappearing out of the room.

Carmen and I play with cars with Milo for another ten or so minutes before he's ready to move on to something else.

"So, is it just me or do you think my sister is pregnant?" I ask Carmen.

"You think so?" she asks, swiveling her head to look at me, her eyes big as she thinks it over.

"She looked exhausted, said she's been feeling randomly nauseous..." I trail off.

"I mean, those can be symptoms, but they can also be symptoms of so many other things, like a stomach bug. I wouldn't jump to conclusions, and don't ask her about it. She might have already tested, for all you know, and it was negative, or maybe she's worried that if she is pregnant that she could end up with another premature baby and all the stress that comes with that. I'm also not the best person to ask, seeing as how I've been around her a whole whopping ten minutes or so," she reminds me.

"Yeah, yeah. As soon as she sat down, I knew something was up," I tell her.

"Well, maybe she'll talk to you about it later. I could see how she might be a little shy to talk to you about anything personal when she's got a stranger in her house."

"Tiffany, shy?" I snort. "If there is one thing my sister isn't, it is shy," I inform Carmen.

"You never know," she sing-songs as Milo hands her another toy.

I sit in amazement as I watch her playing with Milo, and how quickly he's opened up to her. I knew he would quickly fall for her once he got past being shy, but she made it easy for him to do so. Seeing her with him makes me think of how good of a mother she'll one day be. We've briefly glazed over our desire for families of our own. It is obviously way too early in our relationship for us to even be thinking like that, but it's something I could see down the line. While Carmen is still under the impression, we're just giving this whole relationship thing a trial run, I'm in this for real. I've developed real feelings for her. I hate it when we're apart for more than a few hours and want to spend all my free time with her. I hate the nights and following mornings that we aren't together in the same bed.

Eventually, we'll have to take our relationship public. We've kept it pretty low-key at work, not that the guys haven't known that something was going on since that first night in Toronto. Thankfully, they weren't dicks about it when we were still playing. Now that we're in the off season, we don't see each other all that often. Most of the guys leave town and head back to their hometowns. Even though I'm not from Indianapolis, I'd stay here so that I could be around Milo and Tiffany, even if Carmen wasn't in the picture.

"Hey," Tiffany says, joining us again.

"Hey, feeling better?" I ask quietly.

"I think so, I'm going to try eating something small and see how that goes. How have things been out here?" she asks.

"We played lots of cars, and with about every other toy he's got in here, before I turned on a movie about thirty minutes ago. I think he only passed out within the last couple of minutes," I tell her as I sit on the couch, my nephew passed out between Carmen and me. She's rolled right along with everything so far today, and I couldn't love her more for it if I tried. Seeing how she so easily slides into my family makes me believe that this could be our new normal.

"Sounds like a fun time. Did he ever mention being hungry?" she asks.

"Nope, I think he was too distracted by playing and then the movie," I tell her.

"Okay, let me go find something to settle my stomach and I'll be back."

"Would you like any help or company?" Carmen asks Tiffany.

"Sure." My sister perks up slightly at the offer. I just roll my eyes at her, knowing she's been waiting for a day like today to dish all my embarrassing stories from when we were kids with someone I'm dating. Little does she know, I don't care what stories she can dig up, I want Carmen to know everything there is to know about me. I want her to see that we can make this work between us and that at the end of the day baseball might be my job and livelihood, but it is still only a portion of me.

Carmen slips off the couch without waking Milo up. I snag her wrist before she gets away, pulling her in for a quick kiss. "Only believe half of what she tries to tell you about me." I smirk before she pulls away.

"Only half?" Carmen quips back. "I hope she's got some naked baby pictures somewhere." She chuckles quietly.

"I can show you naked later." I wink at her and she just shakes her head at me.

I watch as she disappears into the kitchen. Unfortunately for me, they are far enough away that I can't listen to what they're saying, so I just have to believe that they're talking all sorts of crap about me, but that's okay, I've been expecting it.

SIXTEEN

CARMEN

"How much do you trust me?" Lucas asks me as we're making dinner together.

I turn to look at him, a little perplexed by his question. "Why...?" I ask, drawing the word out.

"Because I'm curious," he says, sliding a hand along my waist and pulling me into him. "I want to take you somewhere, but I need to know that you trust me before I'll even consider stepping foot into the place."

"I'm so confused, where do you want to take me?" I question, my brows furrowed as I try and think of where it is he might want to go.

"I can't tell you yet. I want it to be a complete surprise. But as I said, it requires you to fully trust me," he says yet again.

"Okay, I trust you," I say warily, still confused about where it is that he's thinking about.

"Good, after dinner, we're going out. Wear something

skimpy," he says, running the pads of two fingers along my collarbone and down my cleavage.

"Wait, I'm not going to a strip club with you," I deadpan.

"Don't worry, I wouldn't take you to a strip club unless you asked me to. That's too public of a place, anyway. The place I'm taking you is a private place." Now, I'm even more confused. Trust. Private place. Yet he wants me in a "skimpy" outfit. I rack my brain trying to figure it out while we continue to make dinner together, well, until everything is cooking and he picks me up, placing me on the counter and steps between my legs. I instantly wrap them around his hips, pulling him flush against me. His lips find mine in a bruising kiss.

His fingers dig in to my hips, I'm sure tomorrow I'll have little bruises from them. Not that I care, I love the way he can so easily take control of my body, knowing so many ways to bring me to orgasm. After that promise weeks ago that we'd be adventurous in bed together, we've tried so many things I've only ever seen in movies or read about in books. Never in a million years did I think I'd become adventurous with my sex life, but here we are, very satisfied and willing to give most things a try.

"I could eat you and just skip dinner altogether," he says before his lips find the tops of my breasts that are peeking out the top of my V-neck T-shirt.

"As pleasurable as that sounds, you need sustenance to function, so you have to eat something other than just me," I tell him, trying not to moan the words out as he teases my body into a frenzy.

"If you insist," he says, just as the timer goes off, letting us know it is time for the next step.

We sit down, enjoying the salmon, rice pilaf, and sautéed veggies that we made for dinner tonight. I've always enjoyed cooking, but when I'd do so for just me, I wasn't always that fancy, as it felt like a waste to spend all this time cooking when I was the only one enjoying it. But now that I've got a pretty sexy assistant, it makes cooking fun and very much like an extended foreplay session.

"So, if I have to wear something skimpy, what will you be wearing?" I ask Lucas as we finish up dinner and get everything cleaned up. Working together, we're able to get it done fairly fast.

"I'll be wearing some slacks and a button up shirt," he tells me.

"Tie?" I ask.

"Nope," he says, tapping his index finger against the tip of my nose. "Now, go put on something sexy. I want to see all that glorious skin."

I give him one last, quick kiss before I head for my room.

I stand in my closet, looking around at everything I have, trying to decide what is the skimpiest outfit. I don't usually dress all that skimpy, so I don't really have much that, in my mind, fits, so I settle on a little black dress. You can never go wrong with one. This one has a deep V-neck, which works well with my boobs, showing off a nice amount of cleavage without being porn-star exposed. It hits a few inches above my knees and has a small little slit up the back.

I pull out some of my sexiest lingerie to wear, as well, then head to the bathroom to start getting ready.

Without knowing exactly where we're going, but knowing what we're both wearing, I decide to make my makeup a little more dramatic than I normally wear it. A dark, smokey eye and pair it with a bright and bold red lip. I have a feeling that I'll be bringing Lucas to his knees in more than one way tonight, and I am here for that!

With my makeup and hair done in loose curls, I slip my matching bra and panties on, then the dress over top. I can't quite get it zipped myself, so I go in search of Lucas.

"Lucas," I call from the doorway of my room. "I need your help," I tell him before he comes down the hall.

"Fuck me," he growls when he sees me standing in the doorway. "Maybe we should just scrap going out," he says, crowding me until I have no choice but to step backwards into the bedroom.

"Nope, not after it took me this long to put this look together; you're taking me wherever it is that you think we need to go. Then, you can bring me back home and take this off of me," I tell him. "Now, zip me up," I instruct, turning so my back is exposed to him. "Please," I add as an afterthought when I look over my shoulder at him and see the lust burning in his eyes.

"You're going to torture me all night. I'm going to have fantasies of those red lips wrapped around my cock until it finally happens," he says, nipping at my shoulder as he slides the zipper the rest of the way up.

"Mhmmm, I can't wait," I tell him, shifting just enough so my ass grazes his groin. I can feel how hard he is as he presses even more against my ass.

"You are a little vixen, you know that. Now, let's go, otherwise, we won't ever get out of here," he says.

I do my own inspection of him in his tight slacks and button-up shirt that is rolled to the elbows. I don't know what it is about a man in a dress shirt with his sleeves rolled, but damn if it doesn't make my panties wet.

Lucas escorts me down to his car, ever the gentleman who opens doors and waits to close it until I'm settled into the seat. We pull out and into traffic. I still have no clue where we're going and I'm still confused when we pull into the parking lot of what looks like an industrial building. "Ummm, babe. Where exactly are we?" I ask, a little nervous.

"Do you trust me?" he asks again. I turn to face him as best as I can in the car. I do my best to read his body language and facial expressions.

"Of course," I tell him.

"Okay then," he says, and gets out of the car, coming around to open my door. He slides his hand into mine, intertwining our fingers as he leads me to an unmarked door. He enters a code on the keypad, and we can hear the lock disengage. He opens the door, and we walk into a very bland-looking entryway. He enters a code into a second door, but when this one opens, the walls are professionally decorated. The lights are slightly dimmed, and soft music fills the air.

Lucas leads me down the hall, this time pushing open a door into a large room. As soon as I take in this room, I can feel my eyes go wide in shock. We're in a sex club. There are people all around in different stages of sexual positions. I am shocked speechless, at this point, and don't really know where to look or not to look.

"Just breathe," he whispers into my ear, and I suck in a breath.

"Why-what—" I stumble over my words, trying to form a complete sentence. He moves us, positioning himself in front of me with me facing his is back. All I can see is the elaborate-looking wallpaper and the end of a bar. "Why are we here?" I finally get out.

"Because I wanted you to experience something new," he says, "but I also want you to know that we will not be having sex here. I just wanted you to experience what an aphrodisiac it can be to be in a place where sex is so freeing. This room is going to be tame compared to other rooms in this club. The further you get into it, the kinkier it can get."

"And you've come here before?" I ask.

"Once, but don't worry, they are very discrete. The clientele they cater to expects their privacy to be kept. A place like this wouldn't be able to survive if they leaked who comes here," he tells me and all I can think of is the nightmare a place like this would create for a PR company if one of their clients were linked to it. And here I am, the PR manager, and I'm at a freaking sex club with my boyfriend.

"Okay, I'm good now," I tell him.

"We don't have to stay long if you are uncomfortable," he tells me, reassuring me.

"No, I can handle it," I tell him. He leads me to a small booth, letting me slide in before he does the same. A cocktail waitress approaches and takes our order. An ice water for him, since he's driving, and a large glass of wine for me. If I'm going to experience a sex club for the first time, I'm going to need a little liquid encouragement.

"The center stage is set up very much like a strip club, except here, the people on stage strip completely. Sometimes they'll put on a show solo, and sometimes there'll be multiple people. It is up to the performer if they want people to join them and what they'll allow that person to do. If you look around the room, there are smaller alcoves. These are meant to be semi-private places for couples, or people meeting up here to mingle and do whatever it is they want to do. Some people like the thought that other people might be watching them. Then, the doors around the room lead into private rooms and into other parts of the club."

I look around, taking in the room. It is quite large, and has probably twenty, maybe thirty people here.

"Is that who I think it is?" I ask Lucas, pointing toward a man I recognize. He's currently got one younger-looking woman giving him a blowjob while he fondles another woman's breasts, while she goes down on the other girl. It is all so overwhelming, but I also find myself turned on by everything that is going on in this room.

"If you think that it is the bigwig pastor that is always on TV, then you'd be correct. Like I said, discrete. Much like fight club, the first rule of sex clubs is you never speak of it outside of these walls. The members expect their patronage will never be revealed. Take that guy, as an example. If it got out that he was a frequent visitor, and I'm not saying he is, but think of what kind of headline that would be, not to mention what he's probably got at stake that he could lose. Do you think his parishioners would be okay with the fact that he isn't living the life he's standing up there every Sunday morning preaching about? I'm also going to go out on a limb and guess neither one of those women are his wife."

"Why do you like coming here?" I ask, curious why Lucas would enjoy a place like this.

"I've only ever been here once before, as a guest to someone else. It was something I wrote off as a try it once kind of thing, and never expected to come back. But, after our little talk back in Toronto, the idea came to me one day that maybe you should experience something like this and maybe it would help spark something that you hadn't thought about trying. I just want to be clear that we don't ever have to come back here if this place makes you uncomfortable."

"It is interesting, that is for sure, but I don't think that it's for me," I tell him honestly.

"Thank you for trusting me," he says, leaning over and kissing me. "Now, let's get out of here. I have a dress to strip you out of."

He slides out of the booth and I quickly follow. I came, I saw, I don't need a second visit.

SEVENTEEN

LUCAS

Watching Carmen experience the sex club was an experience all on its own. I knew it was going to press her comfort levels, but she handled it like a pro. While I know that it isn't her kind of place to go back to after this visit, it was hot as fuck to see her experience it for the first time. The way she took in what was happening in different parts of the room was a turn on, in and of itself.

I pull into a parking spot and kill the engine. "Shall we?" I ask, squeezing our clasped hands quickly before we pull apart. She's out of the car before I can make it around and open her door for her, something she knows I try and do whenever I can.

I follow her up to her place, more than ready to strip that dress from her creamy body. "Are you mad at me?" I ask once we're inside.

"No, why would I be mad at you?" she asks, and I step into her personal space.

"Because I pushed you outside of your comfort zone," I tell her honestly.

"I could have gotten up and walked out at any point. It isn't like you were forcing me to be there. I chose to stay."

Her hand drops to my belt and I stand still as she unbuckles it, then pops the button on my slacks and pulls down the zipper. She reaches inside my boxers, pulling out my hard cock.

She kicks off her heels and drops to her knees. I watch as her tongue swipes along those red stained lips I've been envisioning wrapped around my cock all night. Her tongue darts out, licking my tip as she collects the bead of pre-cum that leaks from my tip. *Fuck if that isn't the hottest thing.*

I collect her hair, keeping it balled around my fist, so it stays out of her face, as she takes me into her mouth. My cock hits the back of her throat and I have to stop myself from thrusting my hips. Her mouth is almost as perfect feeling as her pussy is when it pulses around me.

My legs start to shake as she works my shaft with her mouth and fist that is wrapped around it. Her other hand tugs at my balls. I let the sensations take over as my body is filled to the brim with complete pleasure. I feel the tingle start at the base of my spine, moving until it is heavy in my balls. I'm so ready to blow at any moment. I'm coherent enough to give her a little courtesy tap as a warning that I'm about to come, and if she doesn't want it down her throat, she needs to move and move now. Like many times before, she doesn't take my warning, and I lose myself in her mouth.

"Fuck, baby," I tell her, pulling her up once she's released my cock. I'm spent, but more than ready to pleasure her. As much as I enjoy her blowing me, my true pleasure comes from making her come. Knowing that I can make her completely shut everything else in life out long enough to let go, even if it is only for a few minutes, it is the highest feeling in the world. "Your mouth is filthy, and I love it," I tell her before I kiss her hard.

"I need you," she pulls back to tell me.

I tug her dress up and run my hand across her pussy. I find the lace of her panties wet, so I slide them out of the way and sink two fingers inside. I drop to my knees and bury my face between her legs. She has to balance using my body to steady herself. Dropping right here in the middle of the room without any furniture next to us probably wasn't the smartest idea, but I wasn't really thinking about more than my face between her legs. Regretfully, I pull back from sucking on her clit and remove my fingers from her channel. I scoop her up in my arms, carrying her down the hall and into the bedroom where I can really make her come apart.

Since we've stopped once already, I take the time to strip her out of all her clothing. No reason to have any of it in my way if I don't have to. I kiss her hard, but quickly move down her body. I lap at each of her nipples for a few seconds before I kiss down to her navel. I swirl my tongue around it, teasing her as I make my way back to her pussy.

With my body expertly positioned between her legs, they're hooked over my shoulders. I slide my finger through her folds, loving how responsive she is to my touch. Sinking three fingers inside this time, just as I flick her clit with the tip of my tongue. Her body instantly starts trembling. The build-up pays off as she easily starts to fall apart as I fuck her perfect cunt with my mouth and fingers. I absolutely love how she falls apart and just lets her orgasm take over. Her limp body tells me she's well into her orgasmic coma stance that happens after a strong orgasm.

I slide up the bed, waiting for her to rouse after coming on my fingers and tongue. My cock has hardened, not that it ever really went soft, and is ready for round two. Gotta love a quick rebound time.

I wait her out, not wanting to move just yet to grab the condom, but knowing that I'll need to grab it before we can move forward.

"How are you feeling?" I ask once Carmen starts to move.

"Like I've never been better." She smiles at me and I can't help but kiss her.

"You like tasting yourself on my lips?" I ask.

"Eh, not my favorite, but I also want to kiss you right now."

"I need to fuck you," I groan into her mouth, my cock throbbing between my legs. Carmen moves quickly, rolling me to my back as she straddles me. I watch my cock as she slides along it, her wetness coating it. "What are you doing?" I ask.

"I'm clean, I know you are, too. You know I'm on birth control. I just want to feel you. With nothing between us," she says as just the tip slides in a few centimeters and then back out again.

"Fuck, Red," I say, pulling her closer so I can kiss her. With my cock lined up at her entrance, I thrust up, completely filling her. The first time I've ever been inside a woman bareback. "Shit, you feel amazing," I grit out. The intensity of being inside her without a condom is a completely different ball game. I've always loved sex, what red-blooded male doesn't, but this takes it to a whole new level.

"That's it, baby, ride my cock," I tell her as I hold on to her hips, helping her to move up and down.

"Yesss," she chants, the word coming out like a moan as she controls our pace, chasing her orgasm. "Right like that," she tells me as I meet her thrust for thrust. I'm close myself, with the additional sensations happening from being bareback for the first time in my life.

I slide a hand from her hip to her clit, applying pressure just as I know she likes it. It doesn't take long and she's exploding on top of me. I can feel her orgasm start to milk my own, and before I know it, I'm slamming my hips up and coming deep inside her.

Carmen collapses forward, her head resting against my shoulder as she sucks in air, attempting to catch her breath.

"Are you okay?" I ask, running a hand down her sweat-slicked back.

"Perfect," she says, sitting up and smiling at me. Her

completely blissed out look is my favorite look of all time. Her skin is glowing, she looks relaxed, and most of all, comfortable in her own skin. I don't think there is anything sexier about a woman than one who is confident and comfortable with herself. If there is anything that Carmen has, it is confidence.

"Yes, you are." I pull her into a kiss. She laughs against my lips as I lazily kiss them.

I ROLL BACK AND FORTH ON A FOAM ROLLER, working out the kinks in my muscles after a hard day in the gym. Being in the off season doesn't mean that I get to slack off, if anything, I work harder to keep my body in shape and ready for the season to come back around.

"I think you should take some yoga classes; it will help with your flexibility," my personal trainer, Dustin, says.

"I fucking hate yoga," I tell him.

"It's either that or dance classes."

"Yoga it is, then," I tell him, jumping up from the floor. I grab the foam roller, placing it back in the bin.

"If you don't want a private class, I can recommend a few good places to check out," he says.

"I'll let you know; I think I know someone with a hookup."

"All right, man. Let me know. Otherwise, I'll see you in two days," he says, as we do the fist bump into a half hug followed by a back slap—man hug thing, then part ways for the day.

I grab a sports drink from the mini fridge, draining half of it as I head out to my car.

"Hello." Carmen's voice booms out of the speakers as I roll down the interstate.

"Red, how's your day?" I ask her, my cock swelling just from the sound of her voice.

"Pretty good, not much going on today. We had a meeting this morning to brainstorm ideas for next season."

"Sounds fun, are you free for lunch?" I ask, taking the exit off the interstate for my condo.

"I was actually going to cut out of work early. Since we're dead, there really isn't any reason for me to be in the office today."

"So, lunch then?" I ask, hoping she will say yes.

"Sure, what did you have in mind?" she asks.

"I'm easy, you tell me what you want," I tell her as I pull into my building.

"I've been craving some tacos; can we do Mexican?"

"If that's what you want, then sure. I'm guessing you have a specific place in mind?"

"Of course!" she exclaims.

"What time are you leaving work? I just pulled into my garage. I need to go shower and get changed, so you have time. I don't want you to feel rushed."

"I can probably leave in the next half hour or so."

"That should be enough time. Do you want to come here when you leave?" I ask.

"I can do that," she agrees.

"See you then, beautiful."

"See you then, charmer." She giggles before we hang up.

I head inside, going straight for the shower. I turn the water on, letting it get nice and hot while I strip out of my workout clothes. I step under the spray, allowing the heat from the water and the pressure to work the tightness from my sore muscles.

Knowing Carmen is on her way, I don't linger too long, washing up so I can be ready when she arrives. I'm still a little shocked that she wants to go out to eat together, as she's still a bit timid with taking our relationship public, so an idea strikes and has me reaching for my cell.

Lucas: Hey, fuckers, you want to meet Carmen and me for some lunch? She wants to go for tacos, said she's got a place in mind.

I shoot off the group text to JJ, Derek and Matt.

JJ: Sounds good, Riley was just trying to decide what we're going to do, so we're in.

Derek: Jillian is always in for tacos and I'm sure I know where Carmen wants to go. Only the best place in town.

Matt: Shit, sounds like I'll be the only single wheel, but tacos. I guess I can sit with a bunch of love birds when tacos and guacamole is involved.

Lucas: Don't worry, Matt, we'll help you find a lady one of these days.

Matt: I don't need your help, fucker. I can find my own damn woman.

JJ: Someone's a little testy. You need to get laid, O'Riley.

Matt: Fuck off. I'm doing just fine in that department. Thank you very much.

Lucas: Okay, I'll let you know once she gets here and we're ready to leave.

I check the time as I slide my watch onto my wrist. I assume Carmen will be here soon, so I head out into the living room and turn on the TV while I wait for her to arrive. As soon as I sit down, my phone buzzes again, so I pull it from my pocket and see my sister's name on the screen.

Tiffany: What are you up to today, little brother?

Lucas: Not much, just waiting on Carmen to go grab some lunch. What's up?

Tiffany: Any chance I could convince you to watch Milo tonight?

Lucas: Sure, what time?

Tiffany: Five thirty-ish.

Lucas: I can do that.

Tiffany: Can you pack a bag and stay the night? Brad just mentioned getting a hotel room for the night.

Lucas: Sure, what's the special occasion? It isn't your birthday or anniversary.

Tiffany: He got a promotion and wants to celebrate. Plus, a night to sleep in a fluffy hotel room and not have to worry about waking up with a toddler for one night sounds glorious right about now.

Lucas: I've got you covered, sis. I'll see you around five, five thirty-ish.

Tiffany: Thanks, Lucas, I really owe you one.

Just as I finish up texting with Tiffany, the app on my phone that is tied to the building's security system is alerting me that someone is buzzing my unit, so I click on it and see Carmen's smiling face on the camera, so I hit the button to let her up.

I walk over to my door, opening it and leaning against the frame while I wait for her to come up the elevator. I can see her as soon as she steps off and heads my way. She's got on skinny jeans, tucked into some riding boots, a fitted T-shirt on, with a jean jacket layered overtop. She looks casual and sexy as all get out.

"Hello, handsome," she greets, running a hand up my chest and around my neck. I lower down, kissing her a little desperately as I wrap my arms around her torso, lifting her off the ground and into my arms. I carry her a couple steps back until we're in my condo and I can slam the door, all without breaking our connection. With the door closed, I pin her against it, grinding my now hard cock against her center.

"Fuck, I missed you," I say against her lips.

"You just saw me a few hours ago." She laughs and runs her fingers through my hair. The touch of her fingers against my scalp sends shivers down my spine. "And how can you already be hard, we had sex this morning."

"That's all you, baby. You do that to me," I tell her, pressing against her pussy again.

"Sex later, right now, I need food," she says, squirming against me as she attempts to get down.

"Fine," I huff, giving her one last kiss before I let her slide down my body. "I invited some of the guys and their women to join us. Figured you might be more comfortable in a group out in public."

"Oh!" she says, looking up at me. "Thanks, although, the thought hadn't even crossed my mind. That and Taco's and Guac is pretty laid back and used to everyone from both the Lightning and the Eagles coming in. I don't think they'd risk losing all that business just to post about one of you being there."

"That's good to know, now, let's go get you fed. My sister texted a little bit ago and asked if I could watch Milo tonight for them so they can have a date night. I need to be there around five," I tell her as I grab my keys before opening the door back up. I follow her out, stopping quick to lock up before we head down to the garage.

"Has she said anything else about not feeling well?

I'm still worried about her," Carmen asks once we're in the car.

"She hasn't, but we can ask her tonight, that is, if you'll come with me?" I ask as I place my hand on her thigh. When Carmen is near me, I can't help but be touching her.

"I could be convinced into coming with you." She winks at me.

"You're a vixen, you know that?" I ask. "Oh, I meant to ask you about the yoga studio that you go to. Do you think I could tag along with you to a class? Dustin mentioned today that he thinks I should start adding in some yoga to my routine."

"I'm sure you can, it is a first come first serve kind of set up. I like the Saturday morning class the best," she says. "You could come with me this weekend."

"It's a date, then."

"A sweaty one. You might not feel it while in the class, but be prepared to be sore afterwards," she warns.

"I think I can handle it," I tell her. "Oh crap, I was supposed to let the guys know when we were leaving, can you grab my phone and text the group chat. Also, let them know exactly where we're going."

I watch as she grabs my phone, pulling up the messages and shooting off the text.

Lucas: Hey, y'all, this is Carmen. Lucas forgot to text before we left. We're on our way to Taco's and Guac. Should be there in under ten minutes.

"Done," she says. "Derek and JJ both texted back they're on their way with family in tow."

"Sounds good, babe."

"That's going to be one full table." She laughs. "I just love Derek and Jillian's girls. They are the cutest ever," she muses. "I'm so glad that he found his way back to Jillian," she adds.

"I heard a little about that, sounds like it was a messy situation."

"Yeah, he messed up. It took Jillian actually divorcing him to get him to realize everything he was going to lose. He was once my loose screw— always had me on my toes —player, about the time he cleaned up his act, JJ was in the press all the time because of what happened with his daughter, and then you landed on my doorstep. I don't know how I keep putting up with you guys." She smirks.

"You know you love the constant ups and downs your job brings you."

"You're right, I do. I'd like it even more if the players weren't so manwhoreish sometimes." She gives me a pointed look.

"Hey, I haven't done anything bad in months," I remind her.

"Keep it that way, mister." She attempts another pointed look but can't hold it very long before she's laughing with me.

"Has your brother gotten dates yet on when he gets to come visit?" I ask as we pull into the parking lot of Taco's and Guac.

"Nothing firm yet. I was texting with Heather and she thinks it was going to be pushed until after the holidays."

"That stinks, but I guess a visit at any time is better than none."

"Exactly," she agrees.

We walk into the restaurant and I look around to see if anyone has beaten us here. I spot Matt in the corner at one of the large booths. "It looks like someone is already here from our party," I tell the hostess, pointing at Matt.

"Go right over," she states, and I escort Carmen. She waves at a couple sitting at a table; the guy looks familiar, but I definitely recognize the woman sitting across from him as Reese Blackwood. The famous country singer.

"Was that who I think it was?" I quietly ask Carmen before we take a seat across from Matt.

"Yep, that was Austin Jones and Reese Blackwood. They're married and have a daughter. She spends all her off time here in Indianapolis with him, since he plays for the Eagles."

"You weren't kidding when you said this place was laid back and people could just go about their lives as if it was normal for them to be here."

"I think that's why so many people from the two teams congregate here. That and the food is killer," she states. "Hey, Matt, how's it going?" she asks him, placing the menu I hand her from the pile on the table. Apparently, she doesn't need one, if that move indicates anything.

"Can't complain. Just trying to plan a trip," he says.

"Oh yeah? Where to?" Carmen asks. I spot JJ and Riley headed our way, the baby carrier in JJ's hand. He's shortly followed by Derek and his wife and two girls.

He's also carrying an infant carrier, as they just had a new boy a few weeks ago.

"Mexico, maybe, or the Caribbean. I don't really care all that much. I just want a beach, the sun and some drinks. Maybe take a fishing charter one day or go out jet skiing. Any of you guys want to plan something together, I just need out of the dreary winter we're getting into."

"A beach sounds good right about now," Carmen muses.

"I wish we could, but this little man," Jillian points at the baby in Derek's arms, "is keeping us from any vacations right now. He's still a little on the young side for me to feel comfortable going anywhere far from home."

"That's understandable. How's life with a newborn?" Carmen asks Jillian.

"Great, just tiring. And now we're outnumbered so things can be a little trickier at times, but the girls have done so good with having a baby brother in the house."

"Aww, I bet they are just the cutest with him. Two little extra mothers."

"I'm sure he won't find that cute when he's a teenager," Derek chimes in.

"Eh, I'm sure he'll give them just as much shit as they give him," JJ states.

"He's got lots of girls to protect, between his sisters and cousin," Riley adds.

"Are you guys ready to order?" a waitress asks, interrupting our conversation. I realize no one else has even attempted to look at the menu, so I let everyone else order while I scan over the options and go with the daily special.

"Hey, are you serious about a vacation somewhere?" I ask Matt as we all chow down on the chips and salsa.

"Yeah, I just need to get out of here for a little while. Need to reset."

"I'll talk to Carmen about it tonight, see if I can convince her that we should go, and then shoot you some ideas on where. We're watching my nephew tonight, so we can do some research once he's in bed," I tell him.

"No convincing necessary," Carmen interjects. "I'm all over some beach time."

I lean over, speaking only loud enough so Carmen can hear me. "I'm already getting hard at the thought of you in a bikini for a week," I tell her, my eyes dropping to my lap. I love the way her cheeks pinken with a slight blush as my words register.

"You're incorrigible. If we go, I'll be bringing my suits that cover the most amount of skin possible, maybe even a full-on wet suit." She laughs. "I don't think you'd like all your friends seeing me in the skimpy bikini you have pictured in your head right now," she whispers and I growl at the thought of other guys getting to see her like that.

"Okay, maybe you're onto something here with the wet suit." I smirk.

We're pulled from our private conversation about bathing suits when our food all arrives. Damn this place is fast and hella good. I can definitely see the appeal to this place.

EIGHTEEN

CARMEN

I step out into the sand, the sun warming every inch of my skin as I soak it all up. The amount of time we scheduled this vacation in should go down in the record books. Just ten days ago this was an idea, and here we are at a resort in the Caribbean.

"Hey, baby." Lucas comes up behind me, his hands sliding along my waist as he pulls me against him. We stand here, looking out at the water from our semi-private beach front. Our room has walk-out beach access, which is amazing. "Ready to go find some lunch?" he asks.

"Yep, and a fruity drink," I tell him as he links his fingers with mine. We casually walk towards the buffet that is set up by the large outside bar.

We grab plates, piling them high with all sorts of things, then make our way to one of the tables in the shade. Lucas waves Matt down as he sees him enter the line to grab his own plate. It ended up just being the three of us that could get away so quickly for this trip.

"You guys get settled in?" Matt asks, sitting down with us.

"Somewhat," I tell him between bites of food. "I unpacked enough to pull out our suits and my cover up. I can do the rest later. The beach and food were calling my name," I tell him.

"Same. That early morning flight kicked my butt. I'm not a morning person."

We casually visit while we finish up our lunches, then make our way back to the beach, finding some lounge chairs to claim as our own for the afternoon.

"Can you help me?" I ask Lucas, handing him my sunscreen.

"Absolutely." He smirks, taking the tube from me. I watch as he squeezes some out onto his hand before setting it on the chair. He rubs his hands together as I remove my cover up. "Fuckkkkk." He groans once he sees me in my bikini. This one isn't all that skimpy, but still shows off all the goods. "You're going to kill me," he says as he starts rubbing the sunscreen on my back. Even with the heat from the sun, my skin still puckers in goose-bumps as he touches me. The shiver that runs down my spine as he slips his fingers beneath the straps of my top, and under the band in the back, has me wishing we had more privacy at the moment.

"Will you too quit eye-fucking each other?" Matt asks from his beach chair on the other side of Lucas's. "I almost feel like we're in a fucked up threesome." He barks out a laugh.

"You can keep your eyes and paws off my woman,"

Lucas tells him, shooting him a death stare, or what I assume is a death stare underneath his sunglasses.

"I need to find myself a woman." He groans.

"Look around, buddy, I'm sure you can find one to have a little fling with over the next few days," Lucas tells him.

"Maybe," Matt says as he looks down the beach. I've noticed a few groups of girls here, for what appears to be bachelorette weekends or just a good old fashion girls' trip.

Once we're both properly sun screened up, we lay back, soaking in the sun. Before I laid down, I moved my chair to be closer to Lucas's. I grab my phone and snap a few pictures of our view, posting one of me lying on the chair with the water out in the view to my Instagram page. *Enjoying paradise for the next few days!* I even flip the camera around and angle myself, so Lucas is somewhat behind and next to me. I snap a picture, loving how relaxed we both appear in it, then shoot it off to Tiffany so she knows we made it here safely and are enjoying our time.

"You playing paparazzi?" Lucas asks as I set my phone back on the chair.

"Just capturing some memories," I tell him.

"Hmmm... I can think of some other memories we can make." He smirks, leaning over to press a kiss to my lips. I cup his cheek, loving the feel of his beard on my palm. He's allowed it to grow out a little longer than he usually keeps it during the hotter summer months, and I have to say, it is quite sexy on him. Feels good between my thighs, that's for sure. "You keep moaning like that and I'll be scooping you up and hauling ass to the room so I can make you moan even louder," he says against my lips.

"And I'm out." Matt groans, standing from his chair. We both turn and watch him walk down to the water, and I can't help but wonder what is up with him lately. He's always been the easy-going kind, but lately it seems like things aren't that way.

"Do you know what's going on with him?" I ask Lucas as he settles himself back on his chair.

"He hasn't said anything specific, but from the few comments he has made, I think he's tired of the single life. He's one of those guys that really wants to settle down and have a family, but it just hasn't happened for him yet."

"Poor guy," I pout on his behalf. "He's such a nice guy and deserves to find a woman that will make him happy."

"Yeah," Lucas agrees. "Maybe it will happen on this trip," he says, pointing to where Matt is down at the water, talking to a woman and what looks to be her young son. From this distance, I'd say he's probably five or so, based on his size, if I had to guess. I watch as Matt crouches down to the kid's level, the smile that instantly fills his face is noticeable, even from this distance. The kid hands him his ball and Matt steps back some to toss it back to him. We both watch the interaction for a while longer. I almost feel like I'm snooping, so I pull my e-reader out of my beach bag. I get lost in my current smutty read for the next hour or so.

"Want to take a walk?" Lucas asks, pulling me from my book.

"Sure, let me just finish this chapter," I tell him, wanting to know what happens.

It only takes me a couple minutes to finish. I slide my device back into my bag, then slip into my sandals that I'd kicked off earlier. I put my cover up in my bag and sling it over my shoulder. "Can we stop at the room so I can go to the bathroom, first, and so I can drop this off? I don't really want to carry it on our walk."

"Of course," he says, leaning over to kiss me, then takes the bag from my shoulder and carries it for me. We walk up the beach hand-in-hand and straight to our room. After we both use the restroom quickly, I grab two of the water bottles from the mini fridge, downing one before we're even walking back outside.

We walk along the sand, away from the main part of the resort, allowing us to walk where there are less and less people the further down the beach we go. I'd never have imagined, six months ago, that I'd be walking along a beach like this with a man that I'm quickly falling in love with. "Stop here," Lucas says, pulling me to be in front of him, the water and sun behind us. Being late in the after-noon, the sun has started to set and the colors it is creating are just breathtaking. He angles us just perfectly and snaps a picture of us.

"Let me see," I tell him as he turns the phone so I can see the image. I love it. The background, the way he's holding me, the way he's looking at me like I'm the most important thing around. It makes this growing connection feel so real and like it might be something.

He kisses my cheek as we stay in this spot, turned now so we can look out over the water and watch the sun as it slowly sinks closer and closer to the water. "I could get used to watching this every night we're here," he tells me, tightening his hold on me as his chin rests on my shoulder.

"Me too, it is just so peaceful."

We slowly start to head back towards the resort, stopping once we reach the beach area to look for Matt. We don't see him, so we head back for our room to change and get ready for dinner.

The resort has multiple options with both indoor and outdoor restaurants. Since it's been such a laid-back day, we decide to just grab food at the outside bar again. They've got a live band setting up to play, so we snag a table and settle in for the evening.

"Can I get you something to drink?" one of the servers asks as she stops at our table.

"I'll take a Corona," Lucas tells her. "And I'll have the raspberry cosmopolitan," I tell her.

"Right away," she says before returning to the bar top to put in our order.

As soon as she sets them down on our table, I snatch mine, taking a sip of the fruity drink. "All good?" she asks, watching me.

"So good," I tell her, taking another one before I set the glass down.

"Just flag me down if you need anything else."

"Thanks, will do."

"You going to let me get you drunk tonight?" Lucas asks, his hand finding my exposed thigh.

"Maybe, are you going to sex me up tonight if I'm drunk?" I ask, batting my eyelashes at him.

"Red, I'll sex you up anytime you want, all you've got to do is ask." He smirks.

"Hmmm, I like the sound of that," I tell him as the music starts up.

We finish off our dinner and two more rounds of drinks before we join the growing crowd as they dance around while the band plays cover hit after cover hit. A little bit of everything that's on the radio, to please everyone's tastes.

We take a seat back at the table when the band takes a short break. Lucas had flagged down the server on our way over, so she takes our order for another round, plus two bottles of water. With the sun down, it is no longer hot, but still warm out, but add in the alcohol and it is still easy to get dehydrated.

"I wonder where Matt wandered off to this evening," I state, we haven't seen him since we left the beach this afternoon.

"No clue, but he's a big boy and can take care of himself," Lucas replies.

"I know, I just hope he isn't regretting coming with the two of us. We can be a bit nauseating," I tease him. I love the fact that he's comfortable being open with his feelings towards me around his friends and teammates. It makes me feel like that is how things would be if our relationship became public.

The band strikes back up about ten minutes later, and we head back out onto the dance floor for a handful of songs.

"You ready to turn in?" Lucas asks as we sway along to a slow song. He holds me tight, and I love this feeling of being in his arms.

"Yeah, take me to bed," I tell him before pushing up on my toes and kissing him.

I follow behind him as he leads the way back to our room. Once inside, he makes sure the doors are locked and then his attention is on me where I'm sitting on the edge of the large bed.

I track his every move as he closes the distance between the sliding glass door and the bed. He stops just inches in front of me, his button up shirt open and his abs exposed to me. The sun-kissed skin has my mouth watering as I think about the pleasure his glorious body can bring mine.

"What do you want tonight?" he asks, hooking a finger under my chin and lifting my face up to look at him. "Slow and tender or fast and hard?" he asks, his eyes lighting up at his question.

I bite my bottom lip as I think over it. I don't miss how his eyes track the movement of my lip and I know that it drives him crazy, he's only told me at least a dozen times.

"Fast and hard the first time, then slow and tender later," I tell him, knowing damn well that his rebound time is impressive and he's always up for multiple rounds if I am.

"That's my girl," he says. I watch as his shirt hits the floor, followed by his shorts and boxers, which leaves him naked in front of me. His cock is already hard and standing proud. Just seeing it has my mouth watering. I lean forward before he can make a move and lick the tip with my tongue before I suck him into my mouth. The velvety smoothness of his skin against my tongue has my panties wet in no time. I wrap my fingers around the base of his cock as I bob back and forth, taking him as deep as I can without choking.

Lucas collects my hair, holding it out of my way as I suck his cock. I tug at his balls with my free hand, loving the moans and half-spoken curse words falling from his lips as I bring him pleasure. While sucking cock isn't my favorite activity, I'll gladly do it every once in a while, knowing that he gets such enjoyment from it.

"Red," he grits out, tapping my cheek. "I need you to stop, or else I'm going to come," he says as he pulls back. I frown up at him once his cock is free from my mouth.

Before I can say anything, his mouth captures mine in a searing kiss. His arm slips behind me and moves me up the bed, until I'm spread out in the center of it. He breaks the kiss, hovering over me as he takes his fill of me underneath him.

He sits back on his haunches and unbuttons my shorts. I lift my hips, making it easier for him to pull them and my wet panties down my hips and off my legs. While he's doing that, I pull my shirt off, my bra coming off shortly after and all ending up in the pile on the floor, along with his clothes from earlier.

"You are so fucking beautiful," he says, his fingertips ghosting up my torso.

Just as I surprised him with the blowjob, he shocks me when his mouth connects with my clit. The way his tongue circles it, then flicks the bundle of nerves, has my body arching off the bed. He slides two fingers inside, quickly finding my g-spot as his tongue never leaves my clit. It doesn't take him long before I'm falling over the edge and my first orgasm is bringing me immense pleasure.

In my hazy state, I somewhat comprehend that he slides up the bed, lying beside me as I recuperate from the intense orgasm. We've long since had the birth control talk and don't always feel the need to reach for condoms.

He must sense that I'm ready for more, as he rolls me under him and hooks my leg up over his hip. I tug his face down to my own, kissing him as he thrusts into me, filling me completely up.

"Fuck," he says against my lips. "You're so tight tonight." He slowly thrusts a few times, easing us into a faster pace for a few minutes. I tap against his chest and he slows, pulling from my body. I instantly miss the fullness that we just had, but I know that I'll have that feeling back as soon as we switch positions. "What do you want?" he asks, and I push him to the edge of the bed. I roll onto my hands and knees, aligning myself on the side of the bed so he can enter me from behind. He does so, and thrusts in hard, filling me up. His thrust is hard enough, his balls smack forward and hit my already sensitive clit.

"Yes!" I cry out. "More," I tell him, as I can feel my orgasm building once again.

With one hand on my hip and the other on my shoulder, he pounds into me. Every stroke of his cock has my body inching closer and closer to that epic release that it is building toward.

"I need you there, Red," he grits out, and I can feel his cock swelling inside me, his own release on the cusp. I reach down and circle my clit, adding the stimulation needed to have me cresting over the edge. I can't keep myself up, and collapse onto the bed, Lucas still thrusting as I clamp around his cock like a vise. The feeling of his own orgasm hitting him is overwhelming, as he also collapses onto me and the bed.

"Damn, Red. What did you just do to me?" he asks a few minutes later, still attempting to catch his breath. He's pulled out of me, and rolled to the side of me, half on the bed and half off of it so he isn't crushing me.

"I could ask the same of you," I tell him, running my fingers through his hair. I pull him in for a quick kiss, not caring that we're both a sweaty mess.

"I love you," he says, the words so easily slipping from his lips. I still, not really sure if he meant to say them just now or if it is the orgasm talking.

He watches me for my reaction, and I can't help it, tears spring to my eyes as I pull him in tighter. "I mean it, Red. I love you," he tells me again.

"I love you, too," I tell him as I softly cry into his neck.

"Then, why the tears?" he asks, cradling my face as he pulls me back so he can look at me.

"Because I don't know why. You came out of nowhere, were a pain in my ass, then threw the biggest screw ball by being the world's sweetest man when you swept me off my feet and showed me who the real Lucas Black was. Not the one that the press wanted people to believe you were."

"I told you I'd prove them all wrong. You just had to give me a chance."

"And I'll admit that you were right, and I'm glad that I did just that," I tell him honestly.

"How about we go clean up and take a shower, see where the rest of the night leads us," he suggests, his hand connecting with one of my ass cheeks as he gives it a squeeze. I love how comfortable I am with him.

⁂

I ROLL OVER IN BED, THE SUN IS COMING INTO THE room around the corners of the curtains. My body is sore, but oh so worth it. Lucas's stamina puts mine to shame. I don't know how I'll ever keep up with him.

Much like at home, I reach for my phone. I stiffen at the number of notifications on my home screen. I quickly unlock my phone and sit up in bed. Once my phone is unlocked, I go to my texts, first, as I have a large number of those, mostly from Carly.

Carly: Ummm not to alarm you but call me ASAP.

Carly: Carmen, I know you're on vacation, probably sexing it up with that sexy man of yours but CALL ME!

Carly: Fine, just check social media. I'll wait for you to come up for air to tell me what you want me to do.

Carly: Seriously, how much sex can the two of you be having? Pictures of you two on the beach and on the dance floor from last night are EVERYWHERE. Hope you weren't trying to keep this a secret after this trip.

Carly: At least nothing bad is being said, everything so far has been positive, so that's a plus!

"Shit!" I say.

"What's wrong?" Lucas stirs next to me, rolling over to face me. He rubs his sleep-filled eyes before pushing up to sit with his back against the headboard. I can't help but take in the scrape marks my nails left in his skin last night. Oops.

"Well, we're public now," I tell him, turning my phone so he can see the string of texts from Carly.

"And that's a bad thing?" he asks, quirking his brow at me.

"No, I just kind of figured we'd get to announce it on our own. I should have been thinking ahead that this place might be a private resort, but that doesn't mean that we've got complete privacy."

He grabs his own phone from the nightstand, unlocking it and tapping on the screen a few times. "What are you doing?" I ask, just as my own phone pings in my hands. I look down and see that he's tagged me on his Instagram and Twitter profiles. I open the notification and see that he's posted the picture he took of us last night while we were on the walk. The one that I instantly fell in love with.

I read over the caption twice, the words melting my heart just a little bit more. *Enjoying paradise with my love. That's right, ladies and gentlemen, I'm off the market and couldn't be happier. Love you, Red.*

"Really, you had to call me Red?" I ask, quirking a brow at him.

"No one knows *why* I call you that." He smirks, and I can feel myself blush. He leans over and kisses me; morning breath be dammed.

I pull away, knowing that I need to at least reply to Carly. Bless her for trying to warn me and take care of things for me.

Carmen: Sorry for missing all of your texts! I don't know why I didn't think ahead to this happening, but we're rolling with it. Go look at Lucas's Instagram. He just made an announcement on his page. Kinda sweet if you ask me. {winky face} I guess I'll keep him.

Carly: Damn, girl! You guys look so happy. And

DAMN! That look he's giving you says he could eat you alive. That man is S-E-X on legs. You are one lucky woman.

Carmen: I won't argue with that. Thanks again for everything! I'm going to go back to being on vacation mode. Let me know if anything else happens.

Carly: Will do! Bring some of that sunshine back to me! I desperately need it!

I click over to my social media pages, checking to make sure that nothing bad is being said. Some of the comments aren't always the nicest. It amazes me how some women will tear down other women in the comments when guys post pictures of their girlfriends or wives. So much for women supporting women. I know that I can't let their petty comments get to me. They don't know me, hell, they don't even really know Lucas, they just think they do. Before closing out, I decided to post the same picture to my own page, tagging him back in it. I don't quite copy his caption word for word, but the sentiment is there.

NINETEEN

LUCAS

I look out the window, the snow-covered ground greets us as we touch down, back home from a week away in paradise. The vacation was a much-needed time away. It solidified my feelings for Carmen, hell, I told her that I loved her, and we made our relationship public.

"Where are we going tonight?" I ask as the plane rolls toward the gate.

"I'm not super picky," she says, and the idea starts forming in my mind that maybe we should broach the subject of moving in together. We spend most nights with each other as it is, then the week together has me realizing that I don't want to be away from her at night. I've grown accustomed to having her in my arms in bed. Waking up with her every morning. I don't know that I can go back to not having that.

We grab our things, walking off the plane and out to my car. We both packed fairly light, only taking a suitcase each that could fit in the overhead bin. It wasn't like we needed much for clothing. We spent most of the time in bathing suits or shorts and tank tops.

I drive us to my condo, both of us making our way upstairs quietly. I think we're both tired after traveling today, plus all the fun we packed into the last few days. Not to mention, just how tired you can actually come back from vacation. It's late by the time we get here, the darkness settling in all around us.

"I'm going to take a quick shower before bed. I still feel all grimy from the morning on the beach followed by the flight," Carmen says. I watch as she grabs some clean panties and one of my large T-shirts she loves sleeping in. I can't say that I hate seeing her in them, and it has my mind rolling forward a few years and what our life together could be like with a few kids running around. I can picture it now, a little girl with her mother's eyes, my nose, and a smile that will have me wrapped around her little baby finger the moment she's born.

"What are you thinking about?" Carmen's voice pulls me from my daydream. I shake my head and blink twice as I look at her, my T-shirt hitting just above her knees.

"You, us," I say, my voice a little gritty.

"And?" she asks, rolling her hand in a motion, asking me to continue.

"When I saw you pull out my T-shirt, it made me think of how much I love seeing you in my clothes," I tell her, tugging her closer to me. I sit down on the edge of the bed, positioning her between my legs. "That thought flashed forward a few years to you in my T-shirt, stretched over a belly, to a little girl with both of our features."

"That's quite the active imagination," she says, running her hand through my hair before her hand comes down to cup my cheek. I turn my face, kissing her palm.

"It might be a dream, but it is one that I want with you," I tell her honestly.

"Me too," she says quietly. If the room hadn't been quiet, I would have missed her confession.

I look up and see tears falling down her cheeks. I quickly wipe them away. "Don't cry, baby," I tell her, pulling her into my lap. "I know that all of those things are down the road. We don't have to rush anything. Hell, it's only been a few months, but knowing that we're both working towards the same end goal is a good thing, right?"

"Yeah, you just keep amazing me, Lucas. I'm so glad you picked me," she says, cupping my cheek. I pull her back on the bed with me and we lazily make out, no need to rush things along.

"You're the amazing one," I tell her. "I had an idea earlier tonight."

"Oh yeah, what's that?" she asks, shifting so we can more easily see one another as we talk in bed.

"What would you say to us moving in together? We're already at one another's places most nights of the week, and to be honest, I hate it when we end up not together at night."

"Yes!" she exclaims. "I don't care how we make it

happen, but my answer is yes." She smiles and I pull her in for another kiss.

"I don't care about the specifics, either. We can keep your place, keep mine, pick a new place altogether. Just as long as I get to come home to you every night, I'll be a happy man."

"We can decide that in the next few days. There are things I like about both of our places, but there is also something exciting about starting a new chapter of our lives in a new place."

"You just tell me where and I'll be there," I tell her, kissing her once more. I snake my hands up under my T-shirt that covers her body, finding her tits bare, but her nipples already hard as I roll them between my fingers.

"Someone not so tired, all of a sudden?" I ask, sitting up to pull my shirt off over my head.

It doesn't take long before we're both naked and I'm sinking inside her heat. I make love to this woman, the last woman I ever plan to be with, the one that has completely snagged me and turned my life around, making me long for the domesticated life.

TWENTY

CARMEN

"I can't believe today has finally arrived!" I jump up and down, the excitement getting to me as I wait for Zach, Heather, and Simon to get here. Their flight is due to touch down any second now. Zach was finally given dates for his leave, and while we completely missed getting to be together over the holidays, I'll take any time I can get with my family.

"Calm down, babe." Lucas chuckles next to me, where he's sitting on the bench outside of security at the airport. I made him bring me here thirty minutes early. No way was I going to risk traffic or an accident making me late to see my brother, sister-in-law and nephew. He gets to see his sister any time he wants, I only get the few weeks a year the military says my brother can be away.

"Calm, I can't be calm," I tell him, bouncing on the balls of my feet.

"You crack me up," he says.

I watch the screen that shows all the incoming and

outgoing flights. As the screen updates, their flight flips from landing to on the ground and I about lose it again. I know that it will still be at least ten minutes, if not more, before they are actually off the plane and out of security, I just can't contain my excitement.

"Babe, look at this place," Lucas says, handing me his phone. We've still been deciding what we're going to do, but have been leaning towards buying a place.

"Oh, I love it," I tell him as I flip through the pictures.

"It's in the same neighborhood where JJ and Derek live," he says. "JJ sent me the listing, as it just went up today."

"Do you want to go look at it? I think listings in that neighborhood go pretty fast," I tell him.

"Yeah, I can shoot a message to our realtor," he says, as I watch the people as they are streaming out of security, hoping that three of them will be the people I want them to be.

"Done. She's going to reach out to the listing agent and get a time set up."

"Perfect. Can you send me the listing?" I ask.

"Already did." He smiles up at me.

"Excuse me, ma'am." I hear a voice behind me that I'd know anywhere. I spin around so fast, almost knocking into my brother. I launch myself into his arms.

"Zach!" I cry. "You're here!"

"We made it!" he says. "Missed you, sis." He squeezes me a bit tighter before setting me down. I pull my sister-in-law and nephew into a hug, taking Simon from her arms and kissing his cheeks once we break apart.

Once I'm done hugging and kissing my family, Lucas stands behind me and I get the formal introductions out of the way.

"Lucas, this is my brother Zach, his wife Heather and their son, Simon. Family, this is Lucas Black." Lucas and my brother do the whole handshake, half hug, back slap routine, before Lucas gives Heather a quick hug. She's a hugger and I warned him of that. He smiles down at Simon, who just looks him over with some big eyes, not really sure what to think of him.

We head to baggage claim, Lucas helps my brother collect their suitcases before we head to the rental car counter. I offered to let them use my car, but they insisted on renting one of their own, just as they insisted on renting an Airbnb for the week. They didn't want to impose and wanted space with Simon to just relax, plus have the ability to cook and not eat out for every meal.

We part ways at the airport, they have to go check into their rental, with plans to meet back up in about an hour for lunch.

"Hey, babe. Shawna just texted that she could show us the house at three, think we can make that work?"

"I think so, if anything, Zach and Heather can come with us."

"Sounds good, babe, I'll let her know."

"DANG, THIS PLACE IS SWEET!" ZACH SAYS AS WE walk through the large house.

"It is, I really do love it," I say.

"So, what do you say, babe?" Lucas asks, coming to stand next to me in the kitchen.

I look at him, then close my eyes and try to picture us here. I can see it. I can see the happiness we can fill this place with, the memories that will surely come. The holiday and fun times with friends and family. The hopefulness of kids one day filling the halls and empty bedrooms this house has. "I think we should do it," I tell him, feeling butterflies take flight in my stomach at the thought of finding the perfect home for us.

"Shawna," Lucas calls out to our realtor, and she comes back into the kitchen.

"Yes," she replies.

"We'd like to make an offer," he tells her and her smile brightens.

"Great!" she exclaims. "Let me grab my tablet out of the car and we can go over all of it now and then I can send the offer off before we even leave the property," she says, and hustles out of the kitchen to grab her things.

We stand around the kitchen counter as she goes over the offer paperwork, filling in the specifics that we request. Outside of the price we offer, we ask for the standard inspections and for a thirty-day close. The listing agent had told her that the sellers were hoping for a quick closing, as this house was being sold in a divorce and they wanted things finalized quickly.

Once the paperwork is finalized, I take one last walk around the place, snapping a few pictures so I can start to brainstorm ideas on how we're going to decorate this large of a house.

"I can't believe the two of you bought a house today!" Heather says as we enjoy a glass of wine after dinner. We've got Simon in the living room while the guys clean up since we cooked.

"I know, it all happened so fast," I tell her as I hand Simon another toy.

"I'm so happy for you, you deserve it. He seems really good for you," she says, nodding her head in Lucas's direction.

"Yeah, I wasn't so sure in the beginning, I actually kind of hated him when he was first called up to the team. He was such a pain in my ass. Always doing stupid shit that was getting him bad press, and I was always having to clean up his messes. Thankfully, he laid low for a while and then I started to see the real him. He's definitely grown on me. How's life on base?" I ask.

"Ugh, I'm so ready to be back stateside," she says. "I know Zach is going to be a career military man, and I completely support that decision, but I just want to be back in the States. I want to be where I can easily jump in the car or on a flight and be around family in a few hours. While I've made some great friends on base, it still isn't the same as being here and getting to come see you, or going home and seeing our parents. Plus, I feel like everyone is missing out on getting to watch Simon grow up."

"How much longer until he should get moved?" I ask.

"Hopefully within the next eighteen months, but that isn't a guarantee."

"Can he put in a request to where he's sent next?"

"That depends. They'll usually tell him three bases that have openings for his rank and job classification, and he can rank them in order of his preference. It does not guarantee that he'll get his top choice, but it is almost always one of those three."

"I don't know how y'all do it, but I have every ounce of respect for you that you do."

"Thanks, we make it work, and I know that he loves the work, so it makes it all worth it at the end of the day."

We both turn toward the kitchen after the laughter that spills from it. I love knowing that my brother and Lucas as getting along so well together.

"Did you have a good time with Zach?" Lucas asks as we lay in bed together.

"Yeah, it was a great week. I can't believe they're already gone," I tell him, a little sad that our time together is already over.

"He was a cool dude. We got along great," he says.

"Yeah, he told me a few times that he approved of you, so you must have made a good impression on him."

"Damn straight I did. I know what it's like being the

brother. I was protective of Tiffany just the way Zach is protective of you."

"I just hope when they get back stateside it is somewhere close by so we can see each other more."

"Why don't you plan a trip to go see them? Could you go when we're at training camp?" he asks.

"Maybe. I usually go for parts of it, or am available to fly out if I'm needed there."

"I'm sure Carly could handle things for a week for you, she seems pretty capable."

"She's great and she's going to go far in her career. I'm lucky to have her on my team," I tell him as I snuggle in a little closer.

"Are you coming to the inspection tomorrow?" Lucas asks. The sellers accepted our offer on the house within hours and things have moved forward quickly.

"Do I need to be there?" I ask. "I hadn't really thought about it, to be honest with you. With everyone here, I was more focused on spending time with them."

"Only if you want to. I figured I'll go so that if the inspector finds anything, I can have him show me so that I can make sure it gets taken care of."

"That's probably a good idea."

"Are you going to start packing up your place?" he asks.

"I guess I should start doing that, huh." I laugh. "We're going to have such mix matched things, at first." I laugh, thinking over what I have and what Lucas has at his place.

"Instead of moving all our furniture in and then

possibly back out, why don't we just both sell off our things and go buy new stuff that we pick out together. Doesn't that sound like a better idea?"

"It does, we just hadn't talked about that yet and I wasn't sure how much more money you wanted to drop right now, seeing as how you wouldn't let me help with the purchase price."

"Babe, we're good. I've got enough money in the bank to cover it. My signing bonus was more than enough, and we can fill it up with lots of furniture and we'll still be good. Quit worrying about money. Before long, you're going to have to get used to the zeros in my bank account."

"I still feel weird that you're paying for everything," I tell him.

"I'm paying for everything because I want to, and I hope that, sooner or later, it won't be considered my money or your money, but ours. Isn't that what we're working towards here?" he asks, cupping my cheek and placing a soft kiss at the corner of my mouth.

"Yeah, it just still wigs me out sometimes."

"I can accept that, as long as you quit worrying about it."

"I'll try," I assure him.

EPILOGUE

LUCAS

8 months later

It has been about seven months since we closed on our house and moved in together. Life has been crazy during those months. Tiffany and Brad had a little girl a few weeks ago. Another full season has flown by, this time, we made it to the World Series and won! I still can't get over the euphoric feeling of hoisting that trophy up. A dream come true.

"Hey, Red," I greet Carmen as I walk into her office. She's still the sexiest woman, and the way she leads a press conference or meeting with her employees makes me love her even more. She's not afraid to take control of the situation and turn it to work the way she wants it to.

"Mr. Black, what can I do for you?" she asks, biting that fucking bottom lip on purpose because she knows what it does to me.

"I've come to pick my girlfriend up; I'm whisking her

away on a tropical vacation and she told me to be here by eleven," I tell her.

"Well, well. Sounds like she's a lucky lady." She plays along, coming around her desk and standing a foot or so away from me. I close the distance, then tug her until there isn't any space between our bodies. I tilt her head up, then drop mine to capture her lips.

"Let's go, I've got plans for you," I whisper against her lips.

"I like the sound of that, but it better not be anything that hits the headlines," she says, and I'm sure she's thinking back to this time last year when we went on vacation and our pictures were posted everywhere, thus taking our relationship public.

"I'll attempt to be on my best behavior."

"I've heard that before." She rolls her eyes at me before stepping away to grab her things. I smack her ass as she walks away, and get a death glare over her shoulder.

"Don't worry, Red. I'll be slapping that ass later tonight." I smirk as her cheeks pinken.

"Don't be so crass," she whisper hisses, looking around to make sure no one is within earshot.

"Get your ass moving and we won't have to wait until tonight," I tell her and mentally calculate how much time until we need to be at the airport.

Unlike last year when we booked a last-minute vacation down in the Caribbean, this year, I planned a special getaway to one of the places Carmen has told me all about as her most desired vacation spot. This year, we're going to the Maldives. We have one of those bungalows that is out over the water. We can jump right into the crystal-clear water from the deck and swim all around.

"I still can't believe that we're going to the Maldives!" Carmen says once we're both settled into our first-class seats on our first flight. With time zones included, it will take us over thirty hours to arrive, so insisting on the first-class seats was necessary. This first flight isn't horrible, as it is just to Philadelphia, but our flight after that is over twelve hours in the air. We need comfort for that one.

We finally make it to our destination, and I can see why Carmen has had this place at the top of her bucket list. It is like nowhere else I've ever been. The water is so clear, you can see the sand like it is above the water.

We're shown to our bungalow, the amenities pointed out, as well as told who to call if we need anything. The resort has concierges on call twenty-four hours a day to aide us with anything we might need.

"Can we get something light to eat?" I ask before the attendant leaves.

"Of course, anything in particular?"

"What do you have that is fast? I think we're hungry and tired," I tell her honestly.

"We can do a charcuterie board with an arrangement of meats, cheeses, and crackers."

"That will be perfect," I tell her before she exits the room.

I find Carmen out on the balcony, looking out over the water. I stand behind her, boxing her in against the railing as I place my arms on it, and my chin on her shoulder.

"It's so much more than the pictures depict. Thank you," she says, placing her hand on my cheek.

"Of course, even if it was a bitch to get here." She laughs as she relaxes into my embrace. "I have them bringing us something to eat."

"Good, I'm starving."

"I figured, then maybe we can relax in the hot tub before bed?" I suggest. We timed things almost perfectly, with arriving in the evening. Hopefully with a good night's sleep, we'll wake up feeling refreshed and then we can have the rest of our time here to really relax and enjoy the place.

I hear the tapping of someone at the door, so I step away, immediately missing the feeling of her body against mine. I open the door and find the concierge there with a large platter. I let her in, and she places it on the two-person table in the room. I pull some cash from my wallet, tipping her generously for bringing this to us so quickly. "Thank you," I say before she turns to leave.

"Please don't hesitate to call us if you need anything else, enjoy your stay."

She leaves the room and I uncover the tray, grabbing a few chunks of cheese and crackers and pop them into my mouth. "Babe, come join me," I call out, filling one of the small plates with meats, cheese and a few nuts.

"Wow, that's quite the spread," Carmen says, grabbing her own plate to fill. We take them out onto the deck, sitting on the edge with our feet hanging off and into the warm water as we watch the sun sink down below the horizon.

"What is it about us and watching sunsets while on vacation?" she asks as we both dig in to the food.

"Not sure, but I can get used to this," I tell her, motioning to all the amazing things around us. The outside lights on the bungalows all start to come on now that it is dark. They light up, allowing people to safely swim in the water surrounding their place at night if they want to.

Once we're both finished, I put our plates aside and tug Carmen into my lap. We sit like that for a while, just enjoying the quiet.

"Ready for the hot tub?" she asks, turning in my arms to look up at me.

"Yep, but only if we get in naked." I smirk.

"Okay." She smirks right back at me. I didn't think she'd go for it, but she surprises me occasionally.

I make sure that we have towels outside and within reach of the tub, then we both strip out of our clothes and sink into the hot water. Once I'm settled, Carmen straddles my lap, my cock going hard as soon as her pussy slides over it.

"Well, hello," I state, gripping her hips as I help her slide over my cock. A quick lift of her hips and she's sliding down my shaft.

"Yes," she moans as she slowly lifts and lowers her hips, ever so slowly riding me. I move my hands to cup her breasts, playing with her nipples as she kisses me hard.

"Take what you need, baby," I encourage her as she chases her own release.

I can tell she's getting close, but also tiring out, so I drop a hand from her breast and pinch her clit. The added stimulation is all that she needed to go flying over the edge. She collapses forward, the exhaustion of the day hitting her hard, along with the orgasm.

As her hips slow, I remove my hand from her clit and thrust up a few times, finding my own release as her body continues to contract around my cock.

I wait a few moments until our breathing has returned to normal. "Babe, let's go wash off and go to bed. You're about to fall asleep in the water."

"Yeah," she agrees, sleepily. I help her stand from the tub, grabbing one of the fluffy towels and wrapping it around her before stepping out and do the same thing. We head straight for the bathroom. I stop only long enough to open our suitcases and grab our toiletry bags so that we can get ready for bed after the shower.

When I join her, she's already got the shower going and is under the spray. I hand over her shampoo, conditioner, and body wash.

"Thanks, I completely forgot about these," she says, a yawn taking over.

"I know, now wash up so you can get some sleep." Even with seats that turned into beds on the flight, it was still sleep on an airplane, so it isn't like we arrived well rested.

We make it to bed, both crashing within minutes of our heads hitting the pillows.

"Let's go, babe," I call out to Carmen as she gets ready. I scheduled a private dinner out in a cabana bungalow the resort has for special occasions. They've helped me plan this entire night, but it all centers around being there for the sunset.

"Coming. Sorry, I was trying to find the right earrings," she says, putting one in.

"You look gorgeous," I tell her for probably the twentieth time.

"Thank you," she says, giving me a quick kiss. "I'm ready now."

"About time," I tease as I link our fingers together and lead her out of our bungalow. We walk down the path to the main resort turning when we reach the T that will take us to our spot for the night. As we approach the cabana, it is all lit up with tiki torches. They've spread rose petals along the walkway, and all over the floor. In the center is a table for two, champagne bucket to the side and a sitting area near the edge that looks out over the water where we can watch the sun set.

"Good evening," our server greets us. "Can I offer you a glass of champagne?" he offers, holding up a tray with two glasses.

"Thank you," Carmen says, taking one of the glasses before he moves it slightly so I can grab the other one.

"Please enjoy the view, we'll serve the appetizers down by the water's edge in approximately five minutes."

"Thank you so much," she tells him again, then takes

another sip of her champagne. I lead her over to the water's edge. My palms start to sweat as I think over the words that have been on my mind since well before we arrived here earlier this week. The ring in my pocket has been burning a hole since I bought it weeks ago, but I knew that I needed something big and grand to take place when I asked her to marry me.

I set my glass down on the small table, grabbing hers and doing the same. I hold her while we look out over the water, until I realize that I've got to do this if I want the pictures to be perfect.

I turn us once more, this time so we're facing one another. I look down in her eyes and see nothing but the immense amount of love she has for me shining back.

"Carmen," I start, my voice cracking slightly as my emotions catch up with me. "I know our start was rocky, it's safe to say you hated me when we first met," I say, and she chuckles. "Thankfully, I pulled my head out of my ass and stopped being childish. I wanted to prove to you that I wasn't the man the media portrayed me to be. I wanted to prove to you I was a man who could be trusted and one who could sweep you off your feet. One that could be trusted to love you and show you the world." I drop to one knee, pulling the ring from my pocket as I do. I open the box and hold it out. I look up at her tearful, yet happy smile, "Carmen Gibson, will you make me the happiest man on this earth and marry me?" I ask as she launches herself at me.

"Yes!" she screams out. I wrap my arms around her,

lifting her up as I stand. My lips somehow find hers, devouring them as I kiss my fiancée for the first time.

We finally break the kiss, and I pull the ring from the box, sliding it onto her ring finger. It fits perfectly and looks damn good on her.

"Holy shit, Lucas. This thing is the size of a baseball," she says, looking at the rock I just placed on her finger.

"Damn straight, baby. Only the biggest and the best for you," I tell her, kissing her once more.

Ready for more Lightning books? Matt O'Riley's finds his HEA in The Change Up, available on your favorite platform!

IF YOU ENJOYED THE SCREW BALL, PLEASE CONSIDER leaving a review on your favorite retailer.

Ryker

San Francisco Shockwaves Book 1
May 19, 2022
Pre-Order on your favorite retailer!
Add on Goodreads today!

Nothing Bundt Forever

Sweet Valley, Tennessee Book 2
July 27, 2022
Pre-order on your favorite retailer!
Add on Goodreads today!

Aiden

San Francisco Shockwaves Book 2
October 20, 2022
Pre-Order on your favorite retailer today!
Add on Goodreads today!

Cocky Doc ~ A Cocky Hero Club Novel

Nothing Bundt Love

SAN FRANCISCO SHOCKWAVES

Ryker

Aiden

ACKNOWLEDGMENTS

To everyone who has supported me, thank you! Thank You for the impact you have made on my life and my writing. Please know that I appreciate you all!

xoxo,

Samantha

ABOUT THE AUTHOR

Samantha Lind is a contemporary romance author. Having spent the first 27 years of her life in Alaska, she now calls Las Vegas home, where she lives with her husband and two sons. She enjoys spending time with her family, traveling, reading, watching hockey (Go Knights Go!), and listening to country music.

Connect with Samantha in the following places:
www.samanthalind.com
samantha@samanthalind.com

Reader Group
Samantha Lind's Alpha Loving Ladies
Good Reads
https://goo.gl/t3R9Vm
Newsletter
https://bit.ly/FDSLNL

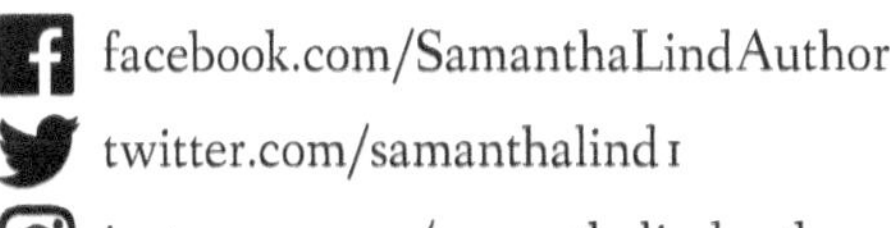

facebook.com/SamanthaLindAuthor

twitter.com/samanthalind1

instagram.com/samanthalindauthor

bookbub.com/authors/samantha-lind